There was a room of alabaster walls with hex signs painted every five feet in brilliant colors. There was a small and ugly child sitting in a black leather chair, and four men standing behind him.

The child looked up, his eyes and lips all but hidden by the wrinkles of a century of life, by gray and gravelike flesh. There was the glint of babyhood close behind that ruined countenance. His voice cracked like papyrus unrolled for the first time in millennia, and he gripped the chair as the words came, "You're the one."

For the first time in many years, I was afraid with a deep and relentless uneasiness that was far more threatening than The Fear which rose in me most nights when I considered my origin and the pocket of the plastic womb from which I came.

"You," the child said again. "I don't like you. You're going to be sorry you came here. I'm going to see to that."

I looked at him. And within my soul I knew that in all the far reaches of the galaxy, to the ends of the larger universe, in the billions of inhabited worlds that might be out there, no name existed for the child. Simply: Child. With a capital.

A DARKNESS IN MY SOUL

DEAN R. KOONTZ

DAW BOOKS, INC.
DONALD A. WOLLHEIM, PUBLISHER

1301 Avenue of tne Americas
New York, N.Y.   10019

COPYRIGHT ©, 1972, BY DEAN R. KOONTZ

ALL RIGHTS RESERVED.

COVER PAINTING BY JACK GAUGHAN.

Dedication:

For G.

PRINTED IN U.S.A.

ONE
Divinity Destroyed...

I

For a long while, I wondered if Dragonfly was still in the heavens and whether the Spheres of Plague still floated in airlessness, blind eyes watchful. I wondered whether men still looked to the stars with trepidation and whether the skies yet bore the cancerous seed of mankind. There was no way for me to find out, for I lived in Hell during those days, where news of the living gained precious little circulation.

I was a digger into minds, a head-tripper. I esped. I found secrets, knew lies, and reported all these things for a price. I esped. Some questions were never meant to be answered; some parts of a man's mind were never intended for scrutiny. Yet our curiosity is, at the same time, our greatest virtue and our most serious weakness. I had within my mind the power to satisfy any curiosity which tickled me. I esped; I found; I knew. And then there was a darkness in my soul, darkness unmatched by the depths of space that lay lightless between the galaxies, an ebony ache without parallel.

It started with a nerve-jangling ring of the telephone, a mundane enough beginning.

I put down the book I was reading and lifted the receiver and said, impatiently perhaps, "Hello?"

"Simeon?" the distant voice asked. He pronounced it correctly—Sim-ee-on.

It was Harry Kelly, sounding bedraggled and bewildered, two things he never was. I recognized his voice because it had been—in years past—the only sound of sanity and understanding in a world of wildly gabbling self-seekers and power-mongers. I esped out and saw him standing in a room that was strange to me, nervously drumming his fingers on the top of a simulated oak desk. The desk was studded with a complex panel of controls, three telephones, and three-dimensional television screens for monitoring interoffice activity—the work space of someone of more than a little importance.

"What is it, Harry?"

"Sim, I have another job for you. If you want it, that is. You don't have to take it if you're already wrapped up in something private."

He had long ago given up his legal practice to act as my agent, and he could be counted on for at least one call a week like this. Yet there was a hollow anxiety in his tone which made me uncomfortable. I could have touched deeper into his mind, stirred through the pudding of his thoughts and discovered the trouble. But he was the one person in the world I would not esp for purely personal reasons. He had earned his sanctity, and he would never have to worry about losing it.

"Why so nervous? What kind of job?"

"Plenty of money," he said. "Look, Sim, I know how much you hate these tawdry little government contracts. If you take this job, you're not going to need money for a long while. You won't have to go around snooping through a hundred government heads a week."

"Say no more," I said. Harry knew my habit of living beyond my means. If he thought there was enough in this to keep me living fat for some time to come, the buyer had just purchased his merchandise. All of us have our price. Mine just came a little steeper than most.

"I'm at the Artificial Creation complex. We'll expect you in—say twenty minutes."

"I'm on my way." I dropped the phone into its cradle and tried to pretend I was enthusiastic. But my stomach belied my true feelings as it stung my chest with acidic, roiling spasms. In the back of my mind, The Fear rose and hung over me, watching with dinner-plate eyes, breathing fire through black nostrils. The Artificial Creation building: the womb, my womb, the first tides of my life. . . .

I almost crawled back into bed and almost said the hell with it. The AC complex was the last place on Earth I wanted to go, especially at night, when everything would seem more sinister, when memories would play in brighter colors. Two things kept me from the sheets: I truly did not enjoy the loyalty checks I ran on government employees to keep me in spending money, for I was not only required to report traitors, but to delineate the abnormal (as the government defined that) private practices and beliefs of those I scanned, violating privacy in the most insidious of fashions; secondly, I had just promised Harry I would be there, and I couldn't find a single instance when that mad Irishman had ever let *me* down.

I cursed the womb which had made me, beseeching the gods to melt its plastic walls and short-circuit those miles and miles of delicate copper wires.

I pulled on street clothes over pajamas, stepped into overshoes and a heavy coat with fur lining, one of the popular Nordic models. Without Harry Kelly, I would most likely have been in prison at that moment—or in a preventive detention apartment with federal plainclothes guards standing watch at the doors and windows. Which is only a more civilized way of saying the same thing: prison. When the staff of Artificial Creation discovered my wild talents in my childhood, the FBI attempted to "impound" me so that I might be used as a "national resource" under federal control for "the betterment of our great country and the establishment of a tighter American defense perimeter." It had been Harry Kelly who had cut through all that fancy language to call it what it was—illegal and immoral imprisonment of a free citizen. He fought the legal battle all the way to nine old men in nine old chairs, where the case was won. I was nine when we did that—twelve long years ago.

It was snowing outside. The harsh lines of shrubbery, trees, and curbs had been softened by three inches of white. I had to scrape the windscreen of the hovercar, which amused me and helped settle my nerves a bit. One would imagine that, in 2004 A.D., Science could have dreamed up something to make ice scrapers obsolete.

At the first red light, there was a gray police howler overturned on the sidewalk, like a beached whale. Its stubby nose had smashed through the display window of a small clothing store, and the dome light was still swiveling. A thin trail of exhaust fumes rose from the bent tailpipe, curled upwards into the cold air. There were more than twenty uniformed coppers positioned around the intersection, though there seemed to be no present danger. The snow was tramped and scuffed, as if there had been a major conflagration, though the antagonists had disappeared. I was motioned through by a stern-faced bull in a fur-collared fatigue jacket, and I obeyed. None of them looked in the mood to satisfy the curiosity of a passing motorist, or even to let me pause long enough to scan their minds and find the answer without their knowledge.

I arrived at the AC building and floated the car in for a Marine attendant to park. As I slid out and he slid in, I asked, "Know anything about the howler on Seventh? Turned on its side and driven halfway into a store. Lot of coppers."

He was a huge man with a blocky head and flat features that looked almost painted on. When he wrinkled his face in disgust, it looked as if someone had put an eggbeater on his nose and whirled everything together. "Peace criers," he said.

I couldn't see why he should bother lying to me, so I didn't go through the bother of using my esp, which requires some expenditure of energy. "I thought they were finished," I said.

"So did everyone else," he said. Quite obviously, he hated the peace criers, as did most men in uniform. "The Congressional investigating committee proved the voluntary army was still a good idea. We don't run the country like those creeps say. Brother, I can sure tell you we don't!" Then he slammed the door and took the car away to park it while I punched for the elevator, stepped through its open maw, and went up.

I made faces at the cameras which watched me, and repeated two dirty limericks on the way to the lobby.

When the lift stopped and the doors opened, a second Marine greeted me, requested that I hold my fingertips to an identiplate to verify his visual check. I complied, was approved, and followed him to another elevator in the long bank. Again: up.

Too many floors to count later, we stepped into a cream-walled corridor, paced almost to the end of it, and went through a chocolate door that slid aside at the officer's vocal command. Inside, there was a room of alabaster walls with hex signs painted every five feet in brilliant reds and oranges. There was a small and ugly child sitting in a black leather chair, and four men standing behind him, staring at me as if I were expected to say something of monumental importance.

I didn't say anything at all.

The child looked up, his eyes and lips all but hidden by the wrinkles of a century of life, by gray and gravelike flesh. I tried to readjust my judgment, tried to visualize him as a grandfather. But it was not so. He was a child. There was the glint of babyhood close behind that ruined countenance. His voice crackled like papyrus unrolled for the first time in millennia, and he gripped the chair as the words came, and he squinted his already squinted eyes, and he said, "You're the one." It was an accusation. "You're the one they sent for."

For the first time in many years, I was afraid. I was not certain what terrified me, but it was a deep and relentless uneasiness, far more threatening than The Fear which rose in me most nights when I considered my origins and the pocket of the plastic womb from which I came.

"You," the child said again.

"Who is he?" I asked the assembled military men.

No one spoke immediately. As if they wanted to be sure the freak in the chair was finished.

He wasn't.

"I don't like you," he said. "You're going to be sorry you came here. I'm going to see to that."

II

"That's the situation," Harry said, leaning back in his chair for the first time since he had taken me aside to explain the job. He was still nervous. His clear blue eyes were having trouble staying with mine, and he sought specks on the walls and scars on the furniture to draw his attention.

The child-ancient's eyes, on the other hand, never left me. They squinted like burning coals sparking beneath rotted vegetation. I could feel the hatred smoldering there, hatred not just for me (though there was surely that), but for everyone, everything. There was no particle of his world which did not draw the freak's contempt and loathing. He, more so than I, was an outcast of the wombs. Once again, the doctors who made their living here and the congressmen who had supported the project since its inception could gloat: "Artificial Creation is a Benefit to the Nation." It had produced me. More than eighteen years later, it had come up with this warped super-genius who was no more than three years old but who appeared to be a relic. Two successes in a quarter of a century of operation.

For the government, that's a winner.

"I don't know if I can do it," I said at last.

"Why not?" asked the uniformed hulk the others called General Morsfagen. He was a chiseled granite man with exaggerated shoulders and a chest too large for anything but tailored shirts. Wasp-waisted, with the small feet of a boxer. Hands to bend iron bars in circus acts.

"I don't know what to expect. He has a different sort of mind. Sure, I've esped army staff, the people who work here at AC, FBI agents, the whole mess. And I've unerringly turned over the traitors and potential security risks. But this just doesn't scan like that."

"You don't have to do any sorting," Morsfagen snapped, his thin lips making like a turtle bill. "I thought this had been made clear. He can formulate theories in areas as useful as physics and chemistry to others as useless as theology. But each time we drag the damn thing out of him, he leaves out some vital piece of it. We've threatened the little freak. We've tried bribing him. The trouble is, he has no fear *or* ambition." He had almost said "tortured" for "threatened" but was a good enough self-censor to change words without a pause. "You simply go into his head and make sure he doesn't hold anything back."

"How much did you say?" I asked.

"A hundred thousand poscreds an hour."

It pained him to say that.

"Double that," I said. For many men, the single hundre thou was more than a year's salary in these time of inflation.

"What? Absurd!"

He was breathing heavily, but the other generals didn't even flinch. I esped each of them and discovered that, among other things, the child had given them an almost completed design for a faster-than-light engine which would make star travel possible. For the rest of that theory alone, a million an hour was not ridiculous. I got my two hundred big ones with an option to demand more if the work proved more demanding than I anticipated.

"Without your shyster, you'd be working for room and board," Morsfagen said.

He had an ugly face.

"Without your brass medals, you'd be a street-gang punk," I replied, smiling the famous Simeon Kelly smile.

He wanted to hit me.

His fists made flesh balls, and the knuckles nearly pierced the skin—they protruded so harshly.

I laughed at him.

He couldn't risk it. He needed me too much.

The freak kid laughed too, doubling over in his chair and slapping his flabby hands against his knees. It was the most hideous laugh I had ever heard in my life. It spoke of madness.

III

The lights had been dimmed. The machines had been moved in and now stood watch, solemnly recording all that transpired.

"The hex signs which you see on the walls are all part of the pre-drug hypnosis which has just been completed. After he's placed in a state of trance, we administer 250 cc's of Cinnamide, directly into his jugular." The white-smocked director of the medical team spoke with crisp, pleasant directness, but as though he were discussing the maintenance of one of his machines.

The child sat across from me. His eyes were dead, the scintillating sparkle of intelligence gone from them, and not replaced by any corresponding quality. Just gone. I was less horrified by his face and no longer bothered by the dry, decaying look of it. Still, my guts felt cold and my chest ached with an indefinable pressure, as if something were trying to burst free of me.

"What's his name?" I asked Morsfagen.

"He hasn't any."

"No?"

"No. We have his code name, as always. We don't need more."

I looked back at the freak. And within my soul (some churches deny me one; but then churches have been denying people a lot of things for a lot of reasons, and the world still turns), I knew that in all the far reaches of the galaxy, to the ends of the larger universe, in the billions of inhabited worlds that might be out there, no name existed for the child. Simply: Child. With a capital.

A team of doctors administered the drug.

"Within the next five minutes," Morsfagen said. He had both big hands fisted on the arms of his chair. It wasn't anger now, merely a reaction to the air of tension that overhung the room.

I nodded, looked at Harry who had demanded to be there for this initial session. He was still nervous over the confrontation of the monsters. I tried not to mirror his unease. I turned back to Child and prepared myself for the assault upon his mental sanctity.

Stepping easily over the threshold, *I fell through the blackness of his mind, flailing* . . .

. . . and woke up to white faces with blurred black holes where the eyes should have been.

They mumbled things in their alien language, and they prodded me with cold instruments.

When my vision cleared, I could see it was a strange triumvirate: Harry, Morsfagen, and some unnamed physician who was taking my pulse and clucking his tongue against his cheek like someone had told him doctors were supposed to do when they couldn't think of anything intelligent to say.

"You all right, Sim?" Harry asked.

Morsfagen pushed my lawyer/agent/father-figure out of the way and thrust his bony face down at mine. I could see hairs crinkling out of his flared nostrils. There were flecks of spittle on his lips, as if he had been doing a lot of shouting in rage. The dark blue of his close-shaved whiskers seemed like needles waiting to thrust out of his tight pores. "What happened? What's wrong? You don't get paid without results."

"I wasn't prepared for what I found," I said. "Simple as that. No need for hysterics."

"But you were yelling and screaming," Harry protested, insinuating himself between the general and myself.

"Not to worry."

"What did you find that you didn't expect?" Morsfagen asked. He was skeptical. I could have cared more, but not less.

"He hasn't any conscious mind. It's a vast pit, and I fell into it expecting solid ground. Evidently, all his thoughts, or a great many of them, come from what we would consider the subconscious."

Morsfagen stood away. "Then you can't reach him?"

"I didn't say that. Now that I know what's there and what isn't, I'll be all right."

I struggled to a sitting position, reached out and stopped the room from swaying. The hex signs settled onto the walls where they belonged, and the light fixtures even stopped whirling in erractic circles from wall to wall. I looked at my watch with the picture of Elliot Gould on the face, calculated the time, assumed a properly bland expression, and said. "That'll be roughly a hundred thousand poscreds. Put it on my earnings sheet, why don't you?"

He sputtered. He fumed. He roared. He glowered. He quoted the Government Rates for Employees. He quoted the Employer's Rights Act of 1986, paragraph two, subparagraph three. He fumed a bit more.

I watched, looking unshaken.

He pranced. He danced. He raved. He ranted. He demanded to know what I had done to earn any pay whatsoever. I didn't answer him. He finished ranting. Started fuming again. In the end, he put it down in the book and vouchered the payment before pounding on a table in utter frustration and then leaving the room with a warning to be on time the following day.

"Don't push your luck," Harry advised me later.

"Not my luck, but my weight," I said.

"He doesn't take to a subordinate position. He's a bastard."

"I know. That's why I needle him."

"When did the masochism arise?"

"Not masochism—my well-known God-syndrome. I was just passing one of my famous judgments."

"Look," he said, "you can quit."

"We both need the money. Especially me."

"Maybe there are other things more important than money."

Someone pushed us aside as equipment was trundled out of the hex-painted room.

"More important than money?"

"I've heard it said . . ."

"Not in this world. You've heard wrong. Nothing's more important when the creditors come. Nothing's more important when the choice is to live with cockroaches or in splendor."

"Sometimes, I think you're too cynical," he said, giving me one of those fatherly looks, something I inherited along with his last name.

"What else?" I asked, buttoning my greatcoat.

"It's all because of what they tried to do to you. You should forget that. Get out more. Meet people."

"I have. I don't like them."

"There's an old Irish legend which says——"

"Old Irish legends all say the same thing. Look, Harry, aside from you, everyone tries to use me. They want me to spy on their wives to see if they have been laying with someone else. Or they want me to find hubby's mistress. Or I get invited to their cocktail parties so that I can perform parlor tricks for a batch of drunks. The world made me cynical, Harry. And it keeps me that way. So, if we're both wise, we'll just sit back and get rich off my cynicism. Maybe if a psychiatrist made me happy-go-lucky and at peace with myself, my talent would disappear."

Before he could reply, I left. When I closed the door behind me, they were wheeling Child down the corridor. His empty eyes stared fixedly at the softly colored ceiling.

Outside, the snow was still falling. Fairy gowns. Crystal tears. Sugar from a celestial cake. I tried to come up with all the pretty metaphors I could, maybe to prove I'm not so cynical after all.

I slid into the hovercar, tipped the Marine as he slid out the other side. I drove into the street, taking the small curb too fast. White clouds whooshed up behind me and obscured the AC building and everything else I put behind me.

The book lay at my side, the dust jacket face down because it had her picture on it. I didn't want to see amber hair and smooth lips imitating a bow. It was a picture that disgusted me. And intrigued me. I couldn't understand the latter, so I pretended to more of the former than I felt.

I turned on the radio and listened to the dull voice of the newscaster casting his tidbits on the airwave waters with a voice uniformly pleasant whether the topic was a cure for cancer or the death of hundreds in a plane crash. "Peking announced late today that it had developed a weapon equal to the Spheres of Plague launched yesterday by the Western Alliance . . ." (*Pa-changa, changa, sissss, sisss pa-changa*, the Latin music of another station added in unconscious sardonic wit) ". . . According to Asian sources, the Chinese weapon is a series of platforms . . ." (*Sa-baba, sa-baba, po-po-pachanga*) ". . . above Earth's atmosphere, capable of launching rockets containing a virulent mutant strain of leprosy which can be distributed across seventeen-mile-wide swaths of territory . . ." (Hemorrhoids really can be dealt with in less than an hour at the Painless Clinic on the West Side, another station assured me, though it faded out before it would tell me how much less than an hour and just how painless.) ". . . Members of the New Maoism said today that they had assurances from . . ."

I turned it off.

No news is good news. Or, as the general populace of that glorious year was wont to say: All news is bad news. It seemed like that. The threat of war was so heavy on the world that Atlas must certainly have had a terrible backache. The 1980s and 1990s, with their general climate of peace and good will made these last fourteen years of tense brinksmanship all the more agonizing by comparison. That was why the young peace criers were so militant. They had never really known the years of peace, and they lived with the conviction that those in power had always been men of guns and destruction. Perhaps, if they had been old enough to have experienced peace before the cold war, their fiery idealism might have been metamorphosed into despair, as with the rest of us. I was very young in the last of the pre-war years, but I had been reading since before I was two and spoke four languages by the age of four. I was aware even then. It makes the present chaos more maddening.

Besides the threat of plague, there was the super-nuclear accident in Arizona which had claimed thirty-seven thousand lives, a number too large to carry emotion with it. And there were the Anderson Spoors which had riddled half a state with disease before the Bio-Chem Warfare people had been able to check their own stray experiment. And, of course, there were the twisted things the AC labs produced (their failures), which were sent away to rot in unlighted rooms under the glossy heading of "perpetual professional care." Anyway, I turned the radio off.

And thought about Child.

And knew I should never have taken the job.

And knew that I wouldn't quit.

IV

At home, in the warmth of the den, with my books and my paintings to protect me, I took the dust jacket off the book so I wouldn't accidentally see her face, and I began reading *Lily*. It was a mystery novel, and a mystery *of* a novel. The prose was not spectacular, actually intended for the average reader seeking a few hours of escape. Still, I was fascinated. Through the chapters, between the lines of marching black words, a face seen at a party weeks before kept drifting through my mind. A face which I had been fighting to forget. . . .

Amber hair, long and straight.

"See that woman? Over there? That's Marcus Aurelius. Writes those semi-pornographic books, like Lily *and* Bodies in Darkness, *those."*

Her face was sculpted, smooth planes and milky flesh.

Her eyes were green, wider than eyes should be, though not the eyes of a mutant.

Her body was graceful, provocatively in vogue.

Her...

I ignored what he was saying about her, all the foul things he suggested, and studied amber hair, cat's eyes, fast fingers touching that hair, clasping a glass of gin, jabbing the air for emphasis in conversation....

When I was finished with the book, I went and made myself some Scotch and water. I am not a good bartender.

I drank it and pretended I was about sleepy enough for bed. I stood on the patio, which is slung over the side of the small mountain which I own, and I watched the snow.

I got cold and went inside. Undressing, I went to bed, nestled down in the covers, and thought about ice floes and blizzards and piling drifts, letting myself find sleep.

I said, "Damn!" and got up and got more Scotch and went to the phone, where I should have gone as soon as I finished the last page of the novel.

I could not understand the logic of what I was doing, but there are times when the physical overrides the cerebral, no matter what the proponents of civilized society might say about it.

Punching out the numbers for directory assistance, I asked for Marcus Aurelius' number. The operator refused to give me her real name and number, but I esped out and saw it as she looked at the directory in front of her: MARCUS AURELIUS or MELINDA THAUSER; 22-223-296787/ UNLISTED.

So I said sorry and hung up and dialed the number I had just stolen.

"Hello?"

It was a competent, businesslike voice. Yet there was a sultriness in it that could not be ignored.

"Miss Thauser?"

"Yes?"

I told her my name and said she would probably know it and then sounded pleased when she did. It was all as if someone were possessing me, directing my tongue against the will of the screaming particle of me that demanded I hang up, run away, hide.

"I've followed your exploits," she said. "In the papers."

"I've read your books."

She waited.

"I think it's time I had my biography done," I said. "I've been approached before, but I've always been against it. Maybe like the primitive tribesmen who feel a photograph locks their soul away inside it. But with you, maybe it would be different. I like your work."

There was a bit more said, and it ended with me and with this: "Fine. Then I'll expect you here for dinner tomorrow night at seven."

I had suggested escorting her to dinner somewhere, but she had said that was not necessary. I insisted. She had said that restaurants were too noisy to discuss business. In the course of the floundering planning, I had mentioned my cook. And now she was coming here.

I went out and swallowed half a glass of Scotch on the rocks (as a change from the Scotch and water), which solved the problems I had just acquired upon hanging the phone on its hook: a dry mouth and a bad case of the chills.

It was stupid. Why be so afraid of meeting a woman? I had met quite famous and sophisticated ladies, wives of men of state and some of them statesmen themselves. Yes, I told myself. But they were different. They were not young and beautiful. That was where the core of my terror lay, though that seemed just as unfathomable as anything else.

At two in the morning, unable to sleep, I got heavily out of bed and walked through the many rooms of my dark house. It is a fine place, with its own theater and gaming rooms, a shooting range, and other luxuries. But there was no solace in seeing all I possessed.

I went into the den and closed the door, looked around without turning on the lights. The machine stood in the corner, silent, monstrous. It was what I had gotten up for in the first place, though I had needed a few minutes to admit it.

The headrest was ominous, a bulky electrode-strung pad that curved to encompass the skull.

But my nerves demanded soothing.

The chair that folded into the machine was like the tongue of some mythical beast, some man-eater and stealer of souls.

I could see the hollow compartment which would swallow me with a single lick, and it terrified me. But I needed soothing. My hands twitched, and a tic had begun in the corner of my mouth. I reminded myself that other generations never had the advantage of a Porter-Rainey Solid-State Psychiatrist and that many people, even these days, could not afford one even when modern technology made it possible. I forced myself to forget the emptiness that would take me later. For the moment comfort was enough. And a few explanations . . .

I sat down in the chair.

My head touched the pad.

The world swiveled up and away, while darkness descended, while fingers probed where they should not be, while my soul was split open like a nut and the meat of my fractured personality was drawn forth for a close examination (in search of worms?).

Proteus Mother taking a thousand shapes, but never to be caught and held to tell the future. . . .

The life spark flickering, then holding steady as a frozen flame. And a very vague awareness even in the womb, where plastic walls were soft and sophisticated thermostatic computers maintained a succor-filled environment. Where plastic walls were giving—but somehow unresponsive. . . .

He looked up into the lights overhead and sensed a man named Edison. He sensed filaments even as his own filament was disconnected from the womb. . . .

And there were metal hands to comfort him. . . .

And . . . and . . . there . . . and . . .

SAY IT WITHOUT HESITATION! The voice was everywhere about me, was booming, was reassuring in its depth of passion.

And there were simu-flesh breasts to feed him. . . .

And . . . and . . .

OUT WITH IT! The computerized psyche-prober immitated thunderstorms and symphonies filled with cymbals.

And there were wire-cored arms to rock him; and he looked out of his swaddling clothes and . . . and . . .

GO ON!

. . . looked up into a face without a nose and with blank crystal eyes that reflected his reddened face. Unmoving black lips crooned, "Rock-a-biiiii-bay-beeeee in theee treeeee (thriddle-thriddle) tops . . ." The thriddle-thriddle rattling interjection was, he found, the sound of voice tapes changing somewhere inside his mother's head. He searched for his own voice tapes. There were none.

GO ON, GO ON!

And he looked up out of swaddling clothes when he esped an understanding and . . . and . . .

IF YOU HESITATE, YOU WILL BE LOST.

I don't remember it after that.
YOU DO.
No!
Yes. YESYESYES. The machine touched part of my mind with blue fingers. Dazzling clouds of neon gas exploded inside my head. I CAN MAKE THE MEMORY EVEN SHARPER.
No! I'll tell it.
TELL.
And he looked up out of swaddling clothes when he esped an understanding, and his first words were ... were ...
FINISH IT!
His first words were: "My God, my God, I'm not human!"
FINE. NOW RELAX AND LISTEN. My electronic David sorted through the miasma of our conversation and interpreted my dreams for me. There wasn't any simple harp music to accompany his readings, though. YOU KNOW THAT THE "HE" IS REALLY YOU. YOU ARE SIMEON KELLY. THE HE OF YOUR ILLUSION IS ALSO SIMEON KELLY. YOUR PROBLEM IS THIS: YOU ARE OF THE ARTIFICIAL WOMB. YOU WERE CONDITIONED FROM CONCEPTION TO HAVE HUMAN MORES AND VALUES. BUT YOU CANNOT HOLD YOUR MANNER OF CREATION UP TO THE LIGHT ALONGSIDE YOUR MORES AND THEN MANAGE TO ACCEPT BOTH.

YOU ARE HUMAN. BUT YOUR MORES TEACH YOU TO FEEL THAT YOU ARE STRANGELY LACKING IN HUMAN QUALITIES.
Thank you. I am cured now and I must leave.
NO. The thunderstorms were firm in their denial. THIS IS THE THIRTY-THIRD TIME YOU HAVE HAD THIS SAME ILLUSION-NIGHTMARE. YOU ARE NOT HEALED. AND THIS TIME I FEEL MORE BELOW THE SURFACE OF THE DREAM, AN ARRAY OF FRAGMENTED TERRORS WHICH SHOULD NOT BE THERE. TELL ME.
There is no more.
TELL ME. The bonds on the chair were tight around my arms and legs. The headrest seemed to suck out the contents of my head.
Nothing.

A WOMAN. THERE IS A FEMININE SPECTER IN THOSE TERRORS. WHO IS SHE? SIMEON, WHO IS SHE?

An author I have read.

AND MET. TELL ME MORE.

Blonde. Green eyes. Full lips like—

SOMETHING MORE.

Full lips.

NO. SOMETHING ELSE.

Let me the hell alone!

TELL ME. It was the voice of a king. The kind who will not have your head lopped off, but who will decapitate you with words and shame.

Breasts. Big breasts that I— That I—

I KNOW YOUR PROBLEM. I CAN SEE, FROM YOUR CONDITION, THAT YOU FIND YOURSELF IN LOVE WITH HER.

No! That's disgusting!

YES. DENIAL DOES NOTHING TO CHANGE REALITY. REFUSAL TO ACCEPT DOES NOTHING MORE THAN MAKE EVENTUAL ACCEPTANCE MORE DIFFICULT. YOU LOVE THIS WOMAN. YET YOU HAVE THIS COMPLEX WHICH ELUDES ME IN ITS ENTIRETY. SIMEON, DO YOU REMEMBER THE SIMULATED FLESH BREASTS?

I remember.

THOSE ARTIFICIAL BREASTS HAVE COME TO SYMBOLIZE YOUR INHUMANITY TO YOU. YOU WERE NOT SUCKLED LIKE A MANCHILD, AND THE LOSS OF THAT HAS DONE STRANGE THINGS TO YOU. YOU ARE AFRAID OF WOMEN, OF—

No. I'm not afraid of women. She was just disgusting. You would have had to see her to understand. All this spoken reasonably, calmly.

NO. YOU WERE NOT DISGUSTED. YOU ARE AFRAID, BUT NEVER DISGUSTED. YOU BACK AWAY FROM EVERYTHING WHICH YOU DO NOT UNDERSTAND IN THIS LIFE. THIS WOMAN IS BUT ONE PART OF THAT. YOU BACK AWAY BECAUSE YOU CANNOT SEE WHERE YOUR PLACE AND PURPOSE COULD LIE IN IT ALL. YOU SEE NO MEANING IN LIFE AND YOU ARE AFRAID TO SEARCH FOR ONE, FEARING YOU WILL EVENTUALLY DISCOVER THERE IS NO MEANING.

THAT IS WHY YOU SPEND SO MUCH, LIVE FASTER THAN YOU SHOULD.

May I go?

YES. GO AND DREAM NO MORE OF PROTEUS MOTHER. YOU WILL DREAM NO MORE. NO MORE... NO... MORE...

It spat me into the room.

After every session with the machine, I was drained, lifeless, some sea creature tossed up on the beach and gasping its respiratory tract raw in a search for the medium of life it was accustomed to. I tossed my fins now, made smacking noises with my mouth, and wiped at my head, which was clammy and cold. I made my way into the bedroom and collapsed onto the mattress without pulling the covers over me.

I tried to encourage pleasant dreams of Marcus Aurelius.

And of Harry. And of money.

But somewhere, quite far way, there was a voice calling to me, a voice which was like chains dragged across a stone floor, like yellowed paper cracking between my fingers. It said, "You're the one they sent for. I know you are. I hate you...."

V

The next morning, there were rumors of military disturbances along the Russian-Chinese border, and news dispatches from the scene said that Western Alliance troops had met in brushfire contact with the Orientals and that a joint report of American and Russian forces would be filed with the U.N. to protest alleged presence of Japanese technical advisors in the Chinese ranks.

The new Chinese horror weapon circling the tired planet had been named Dragonfly by the press. Trust those boys to be original. Or at least colorful. Or, perhaps, just first.

I paid no attention to it. Thus it had been since my childhood, one mini-war after another, one "incident" on the heels of the last, pompous world leaders spouting even more pompous declarations. A man is not constantly aware of his hands. A bird must sometimes forget the sky is there because it has become so familiar to him. Such it is with disaster and war. You can forget as long as it does not touch you, and you can live in better times. It takes a certain peripheral vision deficiency, but that can be mastered with but a small expenditure of time and energy.

I had oranges and tea for breakfast, which helped my headache.

Outside, the city crews had finished cleaning up the snow. The streets were bare, but the buildings and trees were smothered with whiteness. Fences became delicate laceworks. Trees and shrubs were conglomerations of icicles welded together by a frost-fingered artist. A bitter wind swept over everything, stirring the snow, whipping it against the neat houses, the sides of hovercars, and up my nose.

It was as if Nature, via the snowstorm, had tried to reclaim what had once been hers but was now lost to her forever.

Clouds, heavy and gray, betrayed the advent of yet another storm. A low flock of birds streaked north, some kind of geese or other. Their calls were long and cold.

I passed by the broken store window where the howler had lain on its side the night before. It had been removed. There were no police around.

I passed by a church which had burned sometime after I had returned from the AC complex. Its black skeleton seemed leeringly evil.

At AC, the hex signs were on the walls, the lights were dimmed, the machines stood sentinel, and Child was tranced.

"You're late," Morsfagen said. His fists were drawn tightly together. I wondered if he had opened his hands at all since he had stalked out of the room last night.

"You don't have to pay me for the first five minutes," I said. I smiled the famous smile.

It didn't cheer him up much.

I slid into the chair opposite Child and looked him over. I don't know what I expected to have changed. Perhaps it seemed too much to believe that he could go to bed at night and get up in the morning, still in that same condition. It was as if some healing process had to be underway. But, if anything, he looked more wrinkled and decaying than before.

Harry was there. He had worked a third of the *Times* crossword, in ink as he always does, so he must have been there for some while. Like an old woman coming early to mass. "You sure?" he asked me.

"Quite," I said. And I was immediately sorry for having cut him so short. It was the atmosphere of the place, so damned military. And it was Morsfagen. Like Herod—trying to destroy the Child. I was the assassin sent out. And whether my knife was an intellectual or a physical one made no difference, really.

I was on edge for another reason; there was a certain dinner guest this evening....

This time I *parachuted* through the emptiness of his consciousness, no flailing, ready for the drop that awaited me....

... Labyrinth ...

The walls were hung with cobwebs, and the floor was strewn with dirt and bones. The walls were multi-fluted, polished here, rugged here, but a uniform gray everywhere. Far down there, somewhere in the nova-like center of the mind was the Id. It gave out the same, nearly unbearable whine that all Ids do. And somewhere above, in the blackness and the perfect quietude, was the area where the conscious mind should have been. It was clear that the mind of a super-genius was strangely unhuman. Most minds think in disconnected pictures, flittering arrays of scenes and snatches of the past, but Child's mind created an entire world of its own, a realism within his mind, an analogue that I could explore like the actual terrain of some lost land.

There was a clacking of hooves, and from the source of light at the end of the tunnel came the outline in smoke, then the form in flesh of a Minotaur, nut-brown skin and all textures of black hair, eyes gleaming, steam caught in the large ovals of the nostrils.

"Get out!"

I mean no harm.

"Get out, Simeon."

There was a blue field of sparks crackling above his

head, and psychic energies shot thin sporadic flames from his nostrils, the steam to hang there afterwards.

"Leave a monster his only privacy!"

I too am a monster.

"Look at your face, Monster. It is not wrinkled like a dried fig; it is not old beyond its years with seeing; it is not caked with the dust of unlived centuries. You pass for human in your world. You pass. At least, you pass."

Child, listen to me. I am—

He charged and grasped at me with hoof-hands. I fashioned a sword from my own fields of thought and smashed him broadside on the head.

The sound rang in the stone corridors.

My arm reverberated with the force of the blow.

And he was gone, a vapor in the darkness, a phantom.

Holding the green glow of the weapon, I advanced slowly down the twisting halls toward the inner part of him, where his theories would bubble, where thoughts would run in molten rivers. I came out, finally, on an earthen shelf above a yawning pit. Far below, eternities away, drifting and glowing, was a circular mass, and the heat it threw into my face was great.

From here had come the Minotaur. From here came everything.

I reached out and grasped for anything, a subcurrent, a cracked image, the shell of a daydream, and I caught a Hate River ebbing and flowing. HATE, HATE, HATE HATEHATEHATE-HA-TE-HATEHATE HATE . . . Somewhere in the middle of it, a two-headed thing swam, cutting the foul waters with a viciously spined neck. I caught the "T" in HATE and traced it along the currents, searching. T leads ToThumb and a suckling mouTh . . . and The sucking mouTh suddenly To a brown nipple and a moTher's breasT . . . and again The T dominaTed . . . and I allowed The river To carry me ineviTably on Toward Theorem. . . .

Theory Through Tees . . . Through Thousand Times Tedious Tiring . . . Ten Times one Times Two To SuboughT-seven in drepshler Tubes now being used . . .

The flood was too fast. I could see the theory, but I could not divert it fast enough toward the ocean in the distance where a waterspout whirled (taking the thoughts to the little bit of conscious mind he possessed). The thoughts that were now being spoken in dust whispers in a room far away—the thoughts being recorded by serious men with serious faces who listened, no doubt, quite seriously.

Then the drug must have finally taken hold of him, or I would have been swallowed alive by a mind construct and destroyed in his cauldron of insanity. The two-headed beast had swum near without drawing my notice. It caught my eye, now, as it moved swiftly, its mouth gaping, a giant cave that drooled. . . .

I lifted my sword as it raised its huge head above me to strike. Then there was a sudden, jerky slip like an old movie reel that has been spliced, and everything went into slow motion. It was like an underwater ballet. At that rate, it would have taken an hour for the beast's jaws to reach me and snap me up, and I slew him as his red eyes glistened and as a strange THRIDDLE THRIDDLE *came out of his throat. Or hers.*

Turning back toward the river, I directed thoughts toward the slow-moving waterspout until so much time had passed that I thought I had better get out before I lost my own character identity.

I turned away from the screaming Id pit.

I walked back the gray tunnel.

Cobwebs brushed my face.

But there were stairs leading upward this time. . . .

VI

There were candles in her green eyes, reflections of those on the table. The same flickering amber glinted from her hair, made the smooth flesh of her one bared shoulder glow with health. Her sequined, well-cut, Oriental something-or-other was dazzling.

"I'd want nothing held back," she said over the remains of two Cornish game hens of that special diminutive and fleshy mutant strain. Bones and gravy contrasted with her loveliness.

"Nothing," I assured her for the hundredth time.

We sipped the wine, but I felt giddy without it, and her flesh did not need any more glow than it had.

"All your feelings toward Artificial Creation, toward the FBI, and all the others who have used you."

"That could be a blunt book."

"Backing down?"

"Just making an observation."

"Anything watered down would be a flop. Believe me, sensationalism sells a book."

I remembered some passages from *Bodies in Darkness* and smiled and drank my wine and felt my face grow red.

The tape changed. The colored lights playing on the walls to either side ceased. Then a recording of *Scheherazade* came on, and the walls took on color again, spattered with orange, showered over with yellow, bursting with crimson along the baseboard.

She took her wine to the Plexiglas view deck that bubbled out from the east wall of the living room. She stood on the transparent floor of it, as if suspended above the side of the pine-covered mountainside. My mountain thrusts downward into a jumble of shattered rocks, falls off from there into the sea. White waves crashed against the stones below, and a dim echo of the ocean's agony reached us.

I walked after her, forcing myself to be calm, and stood next to her.

The moon was high and full and scarred. My guest was quite beautiful, flushed with its light, but she did not seem altogether real. A woman out of Poe or modeling herself after one.

"I keep thinking of Dragonfly," she said, her eyes up there where it might be.

Toward the horizon a cloud drifted, gray against the purity of the sky. The storm had failed to materialize.

"Why do people enjoy ugliness so much?" she asked. It was such an abrupt change of pace that I was not able to cope with it. I shuffled my feet and smacked my lips at the wine I still held, and tried to think why people did that. She went on without me. "There's all this beauty, and they try to make it ugly. They like ugly movies, ugly books, ugly news."

By then, I was functioning. "Perhaps, in reading about

the worst parts of life, the terrible parts of reality seem more tame by contrast, more easily lived with."

Her lips puckered, as if of their own volition, two separate strips of flesh, entities not a part of her body.

"Truthfully now," she said, "what do you think of my books? You say you've read them."

I was thrown off balance. I had known a couple other writers, and I had never known exactly where criticism should stop and praise begin, exactly how much negative vibration they could take about their work. The last thing I wanted to do was insult or enrage this woman. "Well . . ."

"Truthfully," she said, signaling me that maybe she was tougher than the other artists I knew.

"You mean . . . the ugliness in them?"

"Yes. Exactly." She turned back to the ocean. "I tried writing beautiful books about sex. I gave that up. It's the ugliness that sells." She shrugged her shoulders. Amber hair danced. "One must eat, mustn't one?" Another shrug. Another amber jitterbug.

I was overly aware of the tightness of her bodice.

With the soft light on her face, the vista of the pines and ocean framing her refined beauty with their own rugged majesty, I wanted to grasp her, to draw her to me, hold her, kiss her. At the same moment I felt myself gripped by that desire, I experienced a counter-emotion, a disgust and a deep fear. It was connected to The Fear, to the wombs, to the first moments of my conscious life when I first knew what I was—and what I wasn't.

I brought a hand to that bare shoulder, felt her flesh, resilient and warm, scintillating beneath my fingers.

I took my hand away, breathless and confused.

Turning from her, I began to pace the room, holding my wine glass so tightly that it must surely soon snap in my fingers. I examined the original oil paintings on the walls, as if I were looking for something, though I could not guess what. They had hung here so long that I knew their every detail. There was nothing new in them, not for me.

What did I fear? What about her terrified me so much that I could not bring myself to complete the advance I had made, to draw fingers downwards from her shoulder, to touch the thinly sheathed roundness of her breasts? Was it only what the computerized psychiatrist in the den told

me it was—? Was it only that I feared making too many
contacts in the world and then discovering that I did not
belong? It seemed to me that it ran deeper than that,
though I could not find any other motivations that made as
much sense.

She had turned away from the window, and she looked
at me curiously. I suppose I looked like a caged animal,
prowling that room, sniffing the brilliant canvases for
solace and finding no solace.

I turned and looked at her. But when I tried to speak,
there was nothing to say. I thought, perhaps, in some way
I could never understand, she realized the nature of my
problem more completely than I did.

She crossed the room, her body doing wonderful things
to the clinging black fabric of her dress, and placed a soft
hand upon my lips. "It's getting late," she said.

She took her hand away.

"When do we start?" I asked.

"Tomorrow. And we tape all the interviews."

"Tomorrow, then," I said.

"Tomorrow, then."

And she was gone in a whirlwind of efficiency that left
me standing with my drink in my hand and my "goodbye"
in my mouth like a lump of used lard.

I went to bed to dream . . .

. . . and I woke up needing comfort, a strange comfort
that I could find but one place:

IT IS FOUR O'CLOCK IN THE MORNING, the metal
headshrinker said as it swallowed me and thrust its ethereal
fingers into the pudding of my brain.

I know.

RELAX AND TALK.

*What should I say? Tell me what it is that I could—that
I should say to you.*

START WITH A DREAM IF YOU'VE HAD ONE.

I always have one.

THEN START.

There are storm clouds in the sky: dark, thick, mysterious. There is no place where the sun shows. Below all this piling grayness, beneath the scudding harbingers of rain, there is a hill, a large and rounded hill formed by Nature into a grotesque, gnarled lump, a blemish upon the face of the earth. There are people . . . people . . .

GO ON. The same old urging—*go on, go on, go on....*
There are people ... and there is a cross ... a wooden cross....
FOCUS ON THE CROSS. WHAT DO YOU SEE THERE?
Me.
YES?
Nailed. Blood. Much blood. White, festered wounds dribbling rusty blood around the edges of little holes, neat little holes like the cavities left when you rip the buttons from the faces of rag dolls.... Rusty blood there ...
WHO IS IN THE CROWD?
Harry. I see Harry there. He's weeping.
WHY IS HE WEEPING?
For me.
WHO ELSE?
I'm thirsty.
WHO ELSE?
I'm thirsty. Very thirsty.
THEY WILL GIVE YOU WATER SOON. THEY WILL SLAKE YOUR THIRST. NOW WHO ELSE IS IN THE CROWD?
Morsfagen is casting dice for my cloak. And over there, beyond him, is a pregnant woman who is ...
GO ON, PLEASE.
Please *this time?*
GO ON.
I look at her belly ... and ... there ... is Child. He is weeping too. But he is not weeping for the same reason that Harry is. He isn't weeping for me. It's because he wants up there where I am. He wants out of that woman's womb and up on the cross, nailed and bleeding and thirsty and dying. He wants it so bad that he writhes inside her in fury, wanting out....
DO YOU KNOW WHY HE WANTS OUT?
For the same reason I am happy to be there.
YOU ENJOY BEING ON THE CROSS?
Yes.
WHY?
...
WHY?
I don't know.
DO YOU SEE ANYONE ELSE IN THE CROWD?
No! Oh, no! Oh, my God, my God, my God!

WHAT IS IT? WHAT IS THE MATTER?

No! You'll spoil it/me! I can't! Don't you see my station, my purpose, my nature? It must be my purpose! I haven't got another one, there isn't another one, this must be it! Get away from me! No!

WHAT IS IT? WHO DO YOU SEE?

Melinda. Floating, naked. Floating toward the cross. No! Stay away! You'll spoil my purpose!

STOP IT.

Help! Help me! Don't let her touch me! Forgod'ssake-she'snaked ... naked ... nakednakednakednaked!

STOP DREAMING! WAKE! LISTEN TO ME; HOLD YOURSELF TOGETHER AND LISTEN TO ME.

I—

QUIET. COMPOSE YOURSELF. I WILL INTERPRET YOUR DREAM. THOUGH I MUST SAY THAT THIS THROWS A NEW LIGHT ON YOUR PSYCHE.

DO YOU SEE WHY YOU ARE THE ONE ON THE CROSS? NO NEED FOR AN ANSWER, PURELY RHETORICAL. YOU SEE YOURSELF AS CHRIST—WHAT A NEW DEVELOPMENT!—MORE PRECISELY, AS THE INCARNATION OF CHRIST AS REPRESENTED BY THE SECOND COMING. THERE ARE PARALLELS, OF COURSE, BETWEEN YOUR CONDITION AND THE STORY OF THE CHRIST. YOU COULD SAY THAT YOUR OWN BIRTH WAS A VIRGIN BIRTH, FOR EXAMPLE. YOU WERE NOT CONCEIVED BY FLESH IN FLESH AND THE SPILLING OF SEED, BUT BY THE GENETIC ENGINEERS AND THE COMPLEX CYBERNETIC ARTIFICIAL WOMBS. AND THERE ARE YOUR SUPER-HUMAN POWERS. PERHAPS THEY ARE NOT AS ALL-ENCOMPASSING AS THOSE OF THE CHRIST MYTH, BUT THEY ARE SUFFICIENTLY STRONG TO NURTURE YOUR DELUSIONS.

YOU WERE NOT ABLE TO SEE A PURPOSE TO YOUR LIFE, SO YOU CHOSE TO CAST YOURSELF IN THE ROLE OF A SAVIOUR. IT SERVES A DOUBLE PURPOSE: FIRST, IT REINFORCES ALL YOUR CHRISTIAN MORES, ALL THE THINGS THEY THOUGHT YOU SHOULD BELIEVE AS YOU WERE RAISED (THOUGH THEY WERE AS INTERESTED IN SUPPLYING YOU WITH MORES THAT WOULD KEEP YOU IN LINE AS MUCH AS THEY CARED

ABOUT YOUR HAVING A CHRISTIAN UPBRINGING); SECONDLY, IT GIVES A PURPOSE AND MEANING NOT ONLY TO YOUR LIFE BUT TO THE ENTIRE UNIVERSE WHICH SOMETIMES SEEMS UNEXPLAINABLY CHAOTIC TO YOU—THE WARS AND THE SUFFERING, THE REST OF IT.

I am thirsty.

IN A MOMENT. I MUST FINISH WITH THIS FIRST.

YOU SEE MORSFAGEN CASTING DICE, FOR HE DESPISED AND ONLY USES YOU FOR HIS OWN ENDS. THE CLOAK SYMBOLIZES YOUR LIFE, YOUR PURPOSE, YOUR INDIVIDUAL IDENTITY. THERE SEEMS TO BE A HINT OF THE FUTURE IN YOUR DREAM, A MOMENT OF CLAIRVOYANCE, AND YOU SHOULD BEWARE THE MAN.

Go on.

YOU SEE CHILD AS A THREAT TO YOUR NEATLY BUILT THEORY. HE IS ANOTHER VIRGIN BIRTH, OF THE ORIGIN THAT YOU ARE OF. YOU REALIZE THAT HE HAD BUILT THE SAME SECOND-COMING THEORY TO EXPLAIN HIS OWN PURPOSE IN THE WORLD. YOU UNDERSTAND THAT SINCE HE HAS MET YOU, HIS LIFE PURPOSE HAS BEEN SHATTERED AND THAT HE IS HUNTING FOR ANOTHER ANSWER. YOU DON'T WANT TO HAVE TO DO THAT YOURSELF. YOU DON'T WANT TO HUNT.

THE WOMAN, MELINDA, IS ALSO A THREAT TO YOUR PURPOSE (OR, RATHER, TO THE FANTASY PURPOSE YOU HAVE CREATED FOR YOURSELF). CHRIST COULD NOT FALL PHYSICALLY IN LOVE WITH A WOMAN. BUT YOU HAVE. ADMIT IT. THIS IS YOUR PURPOSE IN LIFE. LISTEN AND KNOW THAT YOUR PURPOSE IS TO LOVE AND COMFORT AND TO BE LOVED IN RETURN. OTHERWISE, YOU FACE ONLY SCHIZOPHRENIA.

Could that be a purpose, though?

IT IS THE OLDEST PURPOSE. WASH YOURSELF CLEAN OF FALSE PURPOSES. ALLOW ME TO ESTABLISH A SERIES OF PERSONALITY TAPES TO REINFORCE YOUR FALTERING SENSE OF REALITY AND TO SUBDUE THIS CHRIST SYNDROME. THE REASON YOU LIVE IS TO LOVE. SO IT IS WITH MOST HUMAN BEINGS. DON'T SEARCH

FOR A LARGE PURPOSE, FOR MORE COMPLEX MEANINGS, FOR THE WHY OF THE WORLD OR THE REASON IN HATE AND WAR. BE SATISFIED THAT YOU KNOW YOURSELF. IT IS A WISE MAN WHO KNOWS HIMSELF.

WE WILL PROCEED WITH THE HEALING NOW....

VII

The following morning, as I stepped out of the elevator near the top of the AC complex, Harry intercepted me before I had taken more than four steps toward the room where Child waited for another session. His round face was drawn, pale, and lined with heavy creases that had not been there before. He looked as if he had not slept all night. A cursory examination of his rumpled clothes and withered shirt collar was proof of that. He grasped my arm, digging his fingers in until it hurt, and steered me across the corridor to an unused office, pushed me inside, followed, and closed the door behind us.

"Cloak and dagger?" I asked. It was amusing to see him engaged in some melodramatic play like this. Yet also terrifying. If Harry Kelly thought there was a need for caution, there most assuredly was. Normally, he had the greatest respect and confidence in due process, even in these days. Many considered him a Polyanna. Now Polyanna was scared, and nothing short of an ogre could have managed that.

"Look, Sim, lay off the arrogance with Morsfagen. Say yes sir and no sir and thank you sir, and help me get his temper down. No smart cracks and no more antagonism. I haven't ever asked you much, but I ask this. Listen, son, it might mean everything we've worked for if you can't keep yourself in check."

"I can't stand the man," I said.

"Neither can I."

"What's happening?"

"The situation is worse than any public communications are reporting it. The Chinese and their Japanese advisors have set up a command post on the Russian side of the Amur River. Only maybe a hundred yards' worth of invasion, but they refuse to move backwards on request. On the Chinese side, troops have been massing for four days. A special spurline was laid down, and troop trains are running in on the hour from the main tracks that pass east of Nunkiang, through the Khingan Mountains."

I took it all in. I'd never been much on geography, and I must have looked rather blank, for he flapped his arms in despair and started on me again.

"On the other side of the border there, the Russian towns Zavitaya, Belogorsk, Svobodnyy, and Shimanovsk lie in a straight line, each within striking distance of the other. Zavitaya contains a missile complex trained on several Chinese population centers. Belogorsk is the site of an extension of the Khabarovsk laboratories, dealing with the problem of lasers. It's the place where the news has been coming from lately—about the possibility of the equivalent of a death-ray. The entire area has become, in the last ten years, a strategic one. If the Chinese can sweep it, they can isolate that arm of the Soviet Union. Toward this end, portable nuke facilities have been moved in on the Amur, pointed toward Zavitaya."

"War," I said. "But we've had it before. And we've been expecting it now for fourteen years or more. Why does this mean I have to brown-nose Morsfagen?"

"I received an interesting telephone call from a judge who was a friend in law school, back in the age of the dinosaur. He reported that Morsfagen has been asking around about the possibility of impounding you—just like they tried years ago."

"We already won that case."

"That was in peacetime. What Morsfagen wants to know is whether the looming war will make a difference."

"Law is law," I said.

"But in time of national crisis, it can be suspended. And the word that the general got, my friend tells me, is that he can pull it off. It will be nasty, dirty, replete with complications—but possible. He'd much rather work with you the way it now stands. But if you drive him to the wall or anger him more than his limit of tolerance, he might decide that its worth a risk to his career. He might try it."

I didn't feel well. I wanted to sit down, but that would have been a sign of weakness. I knew Harry was just barely holding up now. There wasn't any use to make it worse for him. "What's your considered opinion?" I asked.

"The same. Only I think it's more possible for him to succeed than even his own advisors told him."

I nodded. "We'll play it cool, Harry. We'll play it so cool that there will be icicles hanging from the walls. Let's go."

He breathed a sigh of relief and followed me out of the empty office, down the hall, through the door, and into the hex-walled room.

"You're late," Morsfagen said, consulting his watch and scowling at me as he waited for the thrust of my tongue. Maybe he had decided one more witty remark on my part would be the weight to push him to action.

I didn't give him the chance. "Sorry," I said. "I got held up in traffic."

He looked genuinely perplexed, opened his mouth to say something, closed it, and ground his teeth together. It was almost as if he would have preferred being insulted to being treated civilly.

I had come to AC only for the money this time, not to demonstrate my super-humanness, my Christlike talents. The therapy the mechanical psychiatrist had given me had worked deep and had taken root. But with a few more paychecks in my pocket, Melinda and I could be vagabonds for an eternity, running from the ugliness, the filth, war, and the people who made it. I thought of the future in the context of the two of us, though I could not yet know how she felt, whether her interest in me matched mine in her. But from a life of pessimism, I had suddenly become optimistic, and I refused to consider any but the brightest of possible futures.

Child was tranced. His mouth sagged slightly, and his twisted teeth could be seen beyond. His hands trembled against the arms of his chair, even though he was asleep. They administered the drugs while I watched, then stepped back to allow the freaks to converse in the way only we could understand.

I parachuted from the room, down into the labyrinth, not trusting to stairs that might have been there yesterday and not today. . . .

Hooves clacked on rock, the sound like splinters of flying glass.

There was an outline like a child's scrawl, not nearly so definite and real as the day before. Whether he was losing power to refute my presence or merely planning some deception to put me off my guard, I did not know.

There was the vague odor of musk, all the textures of dark hair that fell like night mists, but all of them merely hazy crayon lines.

"Get out!"

I mean you no harm at all.

"And I wish not to harm you, Simeon. Get out."

Yesterday, as you well remember, I fashioned a sword from the very air itself. Do not forget that. Do not underestimate me, though I am in your regions.

"I beg of you to leave. You're in danger here."

From what?

"I cannot say. It is in the knowing that the danger lies."

That is not good enough.

"It is all I can say."

I swung the sword, and he dissipated into an eerie blue vapor that clung to the walls until the wind whistled in to blow it away. It curled along the stone, slithered back to the pit, and was gone.

Two hours into the session, as I was sprawled on the dirt shelf above the pit, grasping at thoughts and diverting them toward the waterspout, a "G" drifted out, and with another level of my mind, I plucked at it and traced it. G to Grass . . . which is dark Green and bendinG over the hills . . . toppinG and hills to see GGGGG . . . G . . . G . . . GodGodGodGodGodGod like a whirlwind moaninG and babblinG over the Glens, cominG, cominG, twistinG relentlessly onward toward me . . . G . . . G . . .

I reached out to take a strong hold on the thought progression, partially because it might lead to something of interest and partially because it was such an odd, intense, and seemingly fractured train of images. Suddenly, the earthen shelf under me gave way, plunging me down toward the flaming pit which sent climbing streams of magma after me.

Wind lifted me toward the river before I could plunge into that cauldron of teeming madness.

I flew as if I were a kite.

The river swept me toward the ocean.

The water there was choppy and hot—and at places steam rose in spirals like smoke snakes.

At places, ice floated, dying.

I fought for the surface, desperately trying to stay on top of the turbulent currents, giving up thought direction and fighting only for the integrity of my own mind. Then I was suddenly up and splashing through the pillar of foamy water that roared into the black, heavy sky; like a bullet out of a rifle, whining, spinning, was I. Splashing, sputtering, I showered out of the mind of Child.

The room was dark. The hex signs glowed on the walls, partially illuminating the serious faces of the generals and the technicians. They were all grimacing, like gargoyle masks.

"He threw me out," I said in the quiet which stretched to the breaking point.

Everyone stared at me with what was obviously a bad case of doubt. I wished I had been more conciliatory in the days past, so that this incident would not appear so suspicious.

"He just threw me out of his mind," I said. It was the first time it had ever happened to me. I explained that. They listened. Somewhere, I was certain, Child was laughing. . . .

VIII

Rumors of war.

The Chinese had slaughtered the skeleton staffs manning the last two Western Alliance embassies in Asia. One was in what had once been called Korea, the other on the home islands of Japan. The Japanese denied any responsibility for the massacre on their own soil. The story was that citizens of Japan and Chinese ancestry had forced their way past the police detailed to protect the Western delegates, had run wild in an orgy of destruction. The Japanese press pointed out that the West, perhaps, should have been expecting this for years, their own silly trade practices—from which China had always been excluded—drawing the wrath of a poverty-stricken people who felt cast aside from the main commerce of the world. Other reports, from eyewitnesses in Japan, said that the Japanese police did not resist the mob at all and actually seemed to be directing its bloodthirsty attack on the foreign consulate offices.

The Tri-D screen showed headless bodies for the benefit of those with shallow imaginations. In the streets of Tokyo, masses marched, holding those heads speared on the ends of sharpened aluminum poles. Dead eyes of our countrymen looked back at us from the other side of the screen. . . .

The Pentagon, the same morning, announced the discovery of the Bensor Beam, which was capable of shorting out all synapses in the nervous system of the human body, leaving the brain imprisoned in a mindless hulk. Named after its creator, a Dr. Harold Bensor, the beam was already being referred to (by Pentagon officials and their cronies in the War Bureau of Moscow) as "the turning point in the cold war." I knew the idea had come from Child; I recognized it the way one recognizes a bad dream that someone has made into a movie. But the censors had learned from the mistakes they had made with me in the past; the public would never hear of Child.

I wondered, for the briefest of moments, what sort of inhuman fiend this Bensor must be to want his name attached to such an inglorious device. Then I lost my façade of superiority when I considered that the weapon might just as likely have been called the Simeon Kelly Beam, for I had been the middleman who had brought it into existence. I was more responsible than anyone, even Child, for whatever might be done with this damn thing.

Pictures on the screen showed two Chinese prisoners on whom the weapon had been used. Spastic, they flopped about on the gray floor of their cell, eyes sightless, ears unhearing, bodies pulled by strings that none of us could really understand.

I turned it off.

I pushed my unfinished breakfast away from me, and got my coat from the closet. I was to meet Melinda at her apartment for another session with the tapes, and I did not want to miss that. Besides, seeing her might somehow purge the strain of guilt running through me.

All the interviews were at her apartment, for she had a ton of equipment there and preferred not to have to move it. That evening, we were going to the theater—and that was no business meeting at all. In fact, even the interviews had become more than business.

I was trying to heed the mechanical psychiatrist's advice, trying to reach out and accept human warmth. And, in small ways, in kisses and touches and a few words, she was returning that effort of mine. To me, so thirsty for companionship after a long drought, it seemed even more heady and fine than it really was.

The sky was gray again and whispered *snow*. It was a regular oldtime winter, a Christmas-card sort of winter, sparkling and white and bitterly cold. Somewhere, far above, floated Dragonfly.

"Did the FBI mistreat you at any other time?" she asked.

The black microphone dangled above us like a bloated spider. Behind the couch where we sat, reels hissed in the recorder, like voices commenting on the anecdotes I told.

"It wasn't the FBI so often as the doctors who treated me not as a human being, but as something to be pricked, punched, and jabbed. I remember once when—"

"Keep remembering," she said. She reached behind the couch and stopped the recorder, laid the microphone down. "That's enough for one day. If it gets moving too fast, you lose the color. You try to tell too much, and the details are blurred. It happens with everyone."

"I guess so," I said.

She was wearing a peasant blouse with a scalloped neckline, an alluring garment which I found myself staring at. And that, in itself, was a shock. It did not seem disgusting, as it once would have. In fact, the fullness, the perfect roundness of her breasts seemed deeply exciting. Perhaps my mechanical psychiatrist had been correct. Perhaps this was a purpose, a legitimate need.

She saw the direction of my gaze. Perhaps that was what produced the following. Perhaps she had been awaiting a sign, and this was the one she saw and chose to travel by. She moved across to the couch, beside me, leaned upwards, and made a bow of her mouth, her tongue flicking along those lips, anxious and inquiring.

What is your mood, the tongue seemed to say. How do you feel? Is this the time? Why don't you do something?

I obeyed the wishes of the tongue. I found it with my lips and with my own tongue, drew her closer with both arms and felt her breasts against my chest. And was not disgusted.

In time, I had touched the flesh of her legs, felt the warmth of her thighs through her skirt. Then I scooped her breasts free of the peasant blouse and tested them with teeth and lips. An hour passed in a minute and had the joy of a century encapsulated in it.

When I left, a hundred yearsa minute later, she stood clean and brown before me, a dark, supple woman divested of all but the glow of her body's youth. We kissed and said nothing more—for there was nothing more to be said. Not really. Even if I could have forced words out of my dry throat.

Outside, I stood in the drive a long while, oblivious of snow and wind, of stares from passing pedestrians, of the need to get to the AC complex and confront Child again. For the first time in my life, I had been with a woman. And she had been a goddess, a good place to start. I didn't feel tainted or used or sinful. I felt better, in fact, than I had ever felt in my life. In time, I managed to think enough to get to the car, climb inside, and close the door. I sat for maybe five minutes before I started it.

My body seemed to burn where she had touched me. Flames played along my lips. All the way to AC...

I was in love: no question. I had not even attempted to esp her thoughts ever since we had met, and that was unusual. I was affording her the same privilege that Harry received, but before she had done half as much for me as he had, before I really knew whether she would accept me or demolish me. I imagine I had been afraid, at first, that she would love me—and later that she would not.

How foolish I had been at the party, weeks ago, when she had been pointed out to me and when, later, she seemed to take interest in me, looking my way, smiling, doing all the things a woman can do. I had bolted. I had left the party even before anyone asked for parlor tricks, and I had hidden in my house, pretending I had not been interested in her. Foolish. I was so much older then—but I am younger than that now.

A band of peace criers had gathered before a precinct

house, for some unfathomable reason. They had stoned the windows. A phalanx of coppers was charging down the steps as I went by.

At a red light two blocks on, a stream of young militants burst from an alleyway to the right, half a block down a side street. They were chanting something, though I could not make out what it was. Behind them, a howler roared into view, its cupola roof narcodart gun cutting down the young people as they cursed the government, the enemy government, and anyone else who came to mind. Before the light turned, I saw the howler roll over a young girl, snapping her back like kindling. That was not standard procedure, by any means. And before I could chalk it up to an accident, the driver of the armored vehicle rammed a boy no older than seventeen, crushed him against the steel pole of an arc lamp, and moved on.

I went through the light to avoid the uproar.

I had to detour around the elevated highway ramp I had intended to use, for there were several hundred people on it, setting up roadblocks in a display of civil disobedience. I noticed that for the first time there were adults with the peace criers. In fact, it seemed that there were more adults than young people.

I took the next ramp, went up, and struck for AC at my top speed. In the time since I had heard the morning news, what could have happened to open the adult ranks like this? My heart beat too fast, and I felt a gnawing urgency to do something, anything. But what?

The only thing I could do was esp Child, find new weapons, make our side stronger so that, if there was a war, we would win and at least a semblance of normality would return in which Melinda and I could carve our own niche and be alone.

I suppose such an attitude was not noble. But war itself leaves no room for nobility. Only the clever survive. And not always do they survive intact.

By the time I reached the government building, I had made my decisions. I loved Melinda. I feared Child. He could throw me out—and perhaps he could swallow me up. There was something behind his repeated warnings to leave his thoughts alone. Something to do with the G association I had chanced upon the day before—something to do with God. I could not sacrifice myself in that strong, mutated subconscious. Yet I could not permit the war and its destruction to touch my life, to end the first warm relationship I had ever had with a woman. Life was only now worthy of living. I could not permit the Chinese to snatch it away from me. So I would go in his mind this last time, rip loose everything that I found and send it up. Then I would get out, collect my cash, and beat a hasty retreat. I would tell them first thing when I got there: after this, the job is ended, go in peace.

As with most plans, nothing went that way.

They were waiting for me when I got there. Morsfagen was the center of a flurry of dispatches. Messengers boys came and departed, carrying sheafs of paper. He signed and checked and rejected, and somehow managed to keep track of what was going on with Child at the same time. Harry fidgeted nervously with his hands, tearing at his fingers as if they were detachable. There were bags under his eyes; the old tic had reappeared in his left cheek; his hair was uncombed.

I esped out to see what was troubling him, breaking the rule which I had established of my own accord. I violated him.

On the surface of his mind, it floated in horrid detail. The thought symbol his psyche had given it was a bloated body floating in a pool of blood. Beneath the image, I read it: WAR. The rumors were not just rumors any longer. Brushfire stuff had gotten hotter, though the details seemed vague in his mind. A black, rotting corpse, floating in clotted pools of blood ...

Extremely shaken, I sat down at the table and looked across at Morsfagen. There were tiny beads of perspiration on his chin and forehead. His big hands were full of communiqués, and they seemed to shiver just the slightest bit.

Damn them! Damn them all!

"The details?" I asked.

"Alliance troops attacked the Chinese division which had crossed the Amur River, drove them back into Chinese territory. Forty-seven Chinese killed. Four Japanese. Seven Alliance troops: two American, one British, and the rest Russian. An hour later, Zavitaya ceased to exist. No radio in or out. The nuke missile site there does not respond to calls. Belogorsk reports a tremor and a play of odd lights in the sky. Seismographs say it was a pocket-bomb, a very low-yield nuke. The troops at the border no longer report back. The Asians have moved into Russian territory with a vengeance. No confirmation yet. But you can bet on it."

"I'll help," I said.

"You're damn right you will." His face was not pretty.

"Is he ready?"

Morsfagen looked at Child. "Tranced," he said. "We were waiting for you before administering the Cinnamide. What have you come up with overnight? What do you think about yesterday?"

I shrugged. "Nothing more than what I've already said. He threw me out because I was reading some thought stream he did not want me to see. It was easy for him, because I never expected it. I was still underrating his potential. I won't do that again."

"Certain?"

"As certain as I can be."

"How is that?"

"Very."

"Let's begin, then."

"Some things have to be done first," I said. "Wake him from the trance. Tell him I have not been here yet. Tell him I've disappeared and that, until I'm found, you'll have to go on without me. Tell him you'll be interrogating him while he's drugged and that he better come across if he knows what's good for him. Ham it up a little. But make it sound convincing. After he is tranced and drugged again, I'll go in secretly. Maybe he won't even know that I'm there."

A black, bloated body (Melinda) floating...

Damn them to Hell!

Morsfagen attended to removing the mutant from the room and going through the procedure I had suggested.

"Are you sure of yourself, Sim?" Harry asked. He sounded as if he wanted me to quit. But we both knew that was impossible. Only Child could develop the ultimate weapon, a weapon that would make war obsolete. I had to go in there until he formulated it—possibly urge him into it if he was unwilling. But there was no backing down— not with the world and Melinda hanging on everything that transpired in this room.

They brought Child back in ten minutes. He was tranced and he was drugged.

The world was heavy on my shoulders and Death was walking with me ...

... and ...

... like a cat with cotton feet, I went quietly, quietly, quietly....

Like a ghost in an old house, I went without form.

Like the breezes of spring, I walked softly.

There was no echo of my steps, and the labyrinth was warmer than usual. The walls were actually unpleasantly hot to the touch, a strange change from the clinging cold that had infested the place. I rounded a bend and saw the Minotaur sitting on his haunches, unaware of my presence. He was reading a leather-bound Bible, completely absorbed in whatever the verses had to tell him.

Slowly, so as to disturb nothing, I passed. He never looked up.

Pasiphaë, here is your unholy child.

Minos, your labyrinth is ugly. It needs a paint job and some common comforts.

Theseus, keep your weapons girdled to your hip, for there will be no killing of a sad and unpretentious Minotaur.

The pit was a tangerine color, pulsating with mind-heat which coursed upwards, washed the rim, flowed down the stone corridors, evicting the leeching cold. The center of the pit was a fierce white dot.

I reached out and grabbed the nearest thought. It was a weapon. But it was nothing that could cure the world's ills, no ultimate dragon as I sought.

A formula to cause ratlike mutations in unborn babies ...

A beam that could dehydrate living tissue, make a living body into a dry, dead corpse in seconds ...

There were many of the G association thoughts, several different progressions of them which led toward one distant point whose nature I could not quite ascertain ...

... an inordinately large number of G thoughts. I was interested in exploring their source and their destiny, but they did not seem to be what I needed.

Then I found it. A stray thought, the ultimate weapon.

F ... Field ... Force Field capable of stopping all entry by anything, including air, permitting neither bombs nor bacteria passage ... Field. ...

I latched onto it and gently nudged it toward the main

stream, toward the waterspout. The ultimate weapon—the weapon to make weapons obsolete.

I thought I was being subtle, but I was underestimating Child. There was a clacking of hooves behind me.

"Get out!"

No. You don't understand.

"It's you who doesn't understand!"

He pounced. I stepped quickly aside, struck at him, and sent him flailing over the brink, into the pit....

Far out at sea, the Force Field Theory was shot up the waterspout. Soon it would be spoken in a dark room, taped, transferred to paper, and sent by special messenger to those who might put it into practice.

Sighing, I turned to go. But with a low, animal grumble, the walls of the labyrinth began to sway and the floor to shake and buck.

From somewhere down in the pit, there was a scream, a deafening ululation which spread throughout the caverns, echoing and re-echoing. Clutching the edge of the pit, the Minotaur was pulling himself onto the earthen ledge. I could see that it was not the Minotaur who screamed, but I could not see anyone else.

What is it? I asked above the noise.

His eyes were wild. He opened his mouth, and I watched horrified as snakes came slithering forth.

I kicked him. He fell back into the pit, all the way to the churning bottom this time.

When I turned back to the caverns, the ceiling caved in before me, dirt and stones spilling over my shoes. And there was no longer an exit. I wasn't going to get out!

I turned to the sea and saw the waterspout dying, withering. There was no hope in that direction, either. No hope! And the situation was so ironic, like Jesus finally sealed into his tomb. But I had given up that delusion, hadn't I?

What, for crissakes, is going on? I yelled above the constant screaming from the pit. Then it occurred to me that I might find the nature of the disaster by latching on to a stray thought. I reached out into the turbulent river and found all of them starting the same way:

G . . . G . . . GGGGGGGGGG . . . *leading*G *to* G*rass rolling over the hills* . . . *to* G . . . G . . . GGG *God God God like a tornado whirling across the Glen, relentless, relentless* . . . GGG GG*od* GG*od* . . . GODGODGOD . . .

random ... what purpose? ... trap Him like the wind to find His purpose, find my purpose ... GGGGGGG. ...

I realized the nature of it then. Child's purpose in life had been shattered when he met me—just as mine had been shattered when I encountered him. He could no longer pretend to himself that he was the Second Coming, the virgin birth. But he had no mechanical psychiatrist to treat him and could find no woman to love or who would love him. He was so restricted in his physical existence that he had to turn to theory and intellectual search to find an answer.

GODGODGODGOD ... trapped in a cavern to tell answers ... GGG ...

I followed the thoughts to their end; I was swept along with them against my will. I never should have listened in the first place. It was the ultimate theory, and he had proven it beyond a doubt....

He had tried to contact God.

He had found the whereabouts of the Supreme Being, the plane of existence upon which He lived.

He asked what meaning there could be to life and to the chaotic world in which man lived. And he was answered; he solved his problem.

He asked what was at the center of creation. And he found out.

And now I was trapped down there.

There were three of us.

Child, Simeon, and God.

And we were all three quite insane.

TWO

Humanity Restored...

I

Trapped within the convoluted miasma of Child's mind, I eventually lost all consideration of what was real and what was not. Here, in the fascinating chiaroscuro ruins of his subconscious mind, the shattered mental analogues were every bit as concrete as the world I had known outside of Child. The stones were textured by the weather as they were in the world beyond; the trees had as many leaves of as many different shades of green as any I had seen before; the wind was not a constant, but changed from bitter cold to almost suffocating warmth, and was moderate more often than not. There were birds and a wide variety of land-bound animals, which, though subtly different or wildly mutated from their "real" parallels, were always believable, detailed and rich with color and habits. At first, I catalogued the differences, the fine points of distinction between the real world and this analogue of Child's interior, but that only made me melancholy, unsatisfied, and soon had me acting like a manic-depressive. I realized that, if this were to be my home for the remainder of my days, I would have to forget the other world I had known. And for my own peace of mind, I would also have to forget that when Child died, we all died, trapped here inside him. It was bizarre, but it was my new reality and required my swift adaptation.

So I adapted.

At first, there had been a time of madness. When I recovered my wits, I did not know how much time had passed, and I could not remember much of what I had done. I remembered running along canyons of stone which shimmered and changed colors around me, thrust up, dissolved, formed new projections, a living rock that sang mournful dirges and sometime burst into long, wailing screams that made me fall and cover my ears and scream in sympathy. There were visions of mottled skies that were sometimes all shades of yellow, sometimes all shades of red, sometimes an ugly whirl of black and brown. I had climbed in cold places and had followed descending trails into warm ones. I had been on strange seas with waters thick like syrup, and in lakes where the surface reeked of brandy. I had seen dark shapes, like huge spiders, dancing along endless webs of sticky white thread, and I had seen maggots crawling in the walls, disappearing in the stone when I came close enough to examine them. At times, a force of monumental strength passed me, a whirling madness of surging energy, which was He, which was God, the maddest of the three of us. And then I was sane, lying on the floors of a wide tunnel, stretched full length, as if I had fallen while running from something that terrified me. I sat up, looked around me, knew that it was so, that I was trapped here, and decided there was nothing to do but make the most of it.

Besides, I nurtured a grain of hope. Perhaps the mind of the wizened boy, this Child, would regain its sanity. Perhaps, then, there would be a way out, a way to return to my own body. They would keep me alive, back there in AC, feed me through my veins, keep my body processes functioning, hoping for my return just as I was. If Child returned to normal, I could go upwards through the now-blocked conscious mind and return to my own flesh. Free. With even the smallest minim of such hope, it was better to maintain my sanity instead of losing it again and being able to return to my own body as a madman.

And, too, there was the possibility that, with my mind intact, I could search out this nightmare landscape and find some chink in the cold stone that kept me from leaving. I could explore for days on end, having nothing better to do, and perhaps discover the passage out. I knew the chances were small. Child's mental analogue was immense, as big as an entire world. It would require years and years just to investigate each corner of it. And a mind destroyed, a mind seeking total refuge from reality, would hardly leave any breach of its seal against the world, no matter how small that breach and no matter in what distant corner it existed.

But I had hope. It was all I had, and it was warmly nourished.

II

Sane and determined, I set out on foot to know the place where I now found myself. There was no need to provision for the journey, no matter what its length, for I no longer held the needs of flesh. There was no such thing as hunger, only a vague memory of what thirst had once been. I couldn't know pain, nor pleasure—except on an emotional, mental level. Though the world seemed physically as tangible as the real one, I moved through it like a spirit, autonomous. I could have formed food and drink from the air—as I had formed that sword to fight off the Minotaur, for I still contained the same level of psychic energy. But it would have been a charade with but a single purpose: to make this world less alien and more like the one I had left. And I had decided that I could only survive by forgetting that other reality and accepting this one fully.

There was no need to rest as I walked, for my analogue body did not tire. I could run, letting the wind whip my hair, for hours on end, without feeling a sore muscle, the tugging fingers of gravity.

I came out of the caves onto a ledge no more than two feet wide that wound out of sight along the side of an immense gray mountain studded with shrubs and gnarled, weathered trees whose extensive roots tangled through the rocks like tentacles. Above, mists obscured the skies, thick roiling masses of gray clouds that moved fast from horizon to horizon. Fingers of the fog came down now and then, slithered along the mountainside, touched the trees and wrapped my legs so that I could not even see my feet.

I walked upward along the trail, deeper into the darkness that lingered there. At places, the trail disappeared, and I had to climb across to where it started again. I feared nothing, for I could not be hurt. As long as Child lived and as long as I was trapped within him, I was invulnerable.

Days or perhaps weeks later, I had gained the summit of the great mountain. It was constructed of four pinnacles, each as tall as a man, which formed, between them, a nest large enough to stand in. I nestled there, hunched over, and looked out across the world that was his tortured mind.

The mists hung all about me and shrouded the path I had walked up on. It was cold and wet and left glistening droplets on my skin. I went naked, though, for cold could not harm me and was not a discomfort. It was merely a quantity now, much like light or darkness. I accepted it and watched the dew bead on the hairs on my arms and legs, like pearls in the shimmering gloom.

I looked out from the peak in all directions. At times, the curtains of gray would part, present a flash of some strange scenery. It was as if all parts of the world were equally near at hand from this summit—but a mile at most. I saw green fields and a silver river cutting through them like the winding body of a python. I saw a cold white plain where there was snow and where slabs of ice jutted upwards like broken teeth. I saw what seemed to be stretches of impenetrable jungle, black flowers blooming on the dark green foliage. I saw endless miles of sand, burnt white beneath a relentless sun, columns of the dried earth stirred upwards into the sky and winding erratically across the barren landscape. There was a land of broken ebony mountains where sunlight was reflected from polished Stygian surfaces and came back brown.

It was clear that I would have to explore all these places if I were ever to find the way out—if there happened to be a way out. I rose from the earth and left the four stone pillars, began the trek down the mountainside once more.

I was a third of the way down when the dark-winged creatures descended through the fog, swept by me, cutting the air with a sharp and unpleasant whine. I looked down where they had disappeared through the lowest layers of the mist. As I watched, they reappeared, rising gracefully toward me. There was a smooth coating of black down over their large, batlike bodies, giving them a warm, smooth, gentle look. Set in each of their faces were two wide eyes, deep brown things which looked back at me with an almost unbearable melancholy.

They settled onto the trail before me, their wings curling in on themselves, rolling into closed scrolls on their backs. Distorted, many-fingered hands reached on tiny arms from the point where their shoulders and wings connected: useless arms.

"Where do you go?" the largest creature asked me.

"To all the lands," I said.

"They are wide. And many."

"I have time."

"That is true."

"Where do you come from?" I asked. I knew they were creatures fashioned by Child's mind, just as he peopled all the landscapes with animals of eerie forms. I was intrigued by their seeming intelligence.

"We are from—from the place where he is trapped."

"Where Child is trapped?" I asked.

"Yes," the smaller one said.

"Why doesn't Child come himself? Why must he take the form of birds?"

"He is trapped. He wants out, but there is no way out except through the dumb animals of his landscapes. He can reach into us and make us more than we once were and thus monitor this land through others' eyes."

"Can you take me to where Child is trapped?" I asked.

"We don't know."

"He can tell you."

"He doesn't know either," the smaller one said.

"Yet both of you are Child," I said. "In essence, you are your master." The wind buffeted us, but we did not mind it.

"I suppose," the larger bird said. "But there's really very little we can do about it. We can help him as he wishes. But he can only impart his general intelligence and psychic power to us. He cannot fully acquire us and speak through us in the direct manner he might wish."

The smaller bird stepped forward and bent conspiratorially. "You are aware, of course, that he is mad. And being mad, he has become separated from total control of this inner world of his. It remains, and he keeps it functioning. But he does not share the harmony of it any longer."

"I understand," I said. "But why did you come to me?"

"We live in the mountains," the larger one said. "While you were here, it was our duty to speak with you about your journey."

"Speak," I said. It was raining slightly, a warm rain.

"We don't know what to say," the large bird said. "We have his general urgency in mind. We understand that he wishes us to say something to you concerning your idea to travel. But we cannot say exactly what he feels about it. We think, ourselves, that he wants you to continue, that he wants us to urge you on. Perhaps he feels that you will find the place where he dwells and will liberate him."

"Possibly," I said.

"We know the place is dark. It is cold and there are things crawling on a blue floor, crawling all around him so that he does not have a moment's peace. That is the sum of our impression."

"I will watch for it," I said. "Now, I must be going."

Without a word, they leaped over the chasm, fell through the mists until their wings buoyed them up, then soared, beyond me, and were gone, making chittering noises like dice rattled on a felt table.

I went down, past the entrance to the inside of the mountain out of which I had come earlier. I walked for another day and reached the tree-shrouded floor of the valley, where the air smelled of pine and of flowers. Waiting for me there was a creature much like a wolf, with a hugely swollen head and a mouth full of long teeth. Eyes like chips of iron, gray and unperturbed.

"I'll guide you through the valley," it said, scratching paws in the earth. "I know it, and I can give you a look at every hole there is."

"Fine," I said.

"First, you must change yourself. Assume my form so that we can go more easily."

I had forgotten that the gossamer body analogue which I had assumed for my journey through Child's mental landscape was not the only shell I could use to contain my psychic energy. There was nothing essential about a humanoid form, for that psychic energy could take any form that I wished. Gently, I released the surface tension of the current, permitted my human body to shimmer and dissipate. I flowed, settled, grew lower and sleeker until I was a double for the wolf that waited for me.

I snuffled, scratched at the earth with razored claws and saw the dirt runnel before me. In this new body, I had a sense of power which I had never experienced before, a new perspective on the world about me. It seemed as if I had been born to lycanthropy.

"Let's go," I said.

The wolf turned and loped away between the thick trees, his big paws scattering dry, brown pine needles which carpeted the forest floor. They rained over me as I hurried to follow his example.

As I ran, my breath steamed in the cold air, and my massive lungs heaved within my chest at the strenuous pace we set.

The ground flashed under me. Flimsy brush parted before me and closed, quivering, behind. To either side, small animals ran, chittering and whimpering with their fear. It was a completely structured reality, and it had made me the king of beasts in this part of the woods. I felt a burgeoning excitement at my omnipotence and my superiority over these lesser creatures. And while I savored this heady attitude, I never once realized the danger that was reaching cold fingers around me.

I enjoyed the muscular rhythm I had never known either as a man or spirit, closed the gap on the wolf, reached it by the time we broke through the pines into a grassy field. We ran side by side, easy, smoothly, sure of ourselves.

The journey had begun in earnest.

III

We prowled the depths of the woods, sniffing through the underbrush for the scent of Child, the odor of his mental essence. There were times when I forgot everything but my powerful shoulders, my claws and my teeth, the keen powers of my black nostrils.

We rooted through the dark cavelets along the valley walls which opened on the floor of the forest, seeking into their darkest recesses, where our eyes refused to be totally blinded. We overturned old, rotting logs in the woods, seeking burrows through which the entrance to Child's prison might be found. We padded through the foaming cascade of a waterfall which issued from the valley rim a thousand feet above, searching the subterranean chambers beyond that wet curtain, finding nothing. If there was a place with a blue floor where Child lay encircled by undescribed creatures of a malignant nature, it was nowhere within this valley. Neither was there a doorway into the conscious mind, no exit from this place where I found myself trapped. The journey was not to have a swift conclusion.

For some reason, I was glad for the extension. There was a strong reluctance to part with the form I had taken, to return to the world and be, again, a man.

It was snowing outside as the wolf led me across the last expanse of open fields before the impenetrable wall of mist which separated this part of the analogue world from the next. Big white flakes clung to our coats and frosted us, kicked up in clouds as we pranced forward toward the distant veil of fog.

We were sidetracked by the scampering of a covey of quail-like animals off to our left. My lupine friend broke into a wild, breathtaking run, teeth bared ferociously, lips drawn back, slobber falling from his wide mouth.

I followed, feeling the wind and snow and scenting the flesh of small creatures.

I saw him leap: muscles taut. I saw him land: a spring's coils jammed together.

The air reverberated with the dying squeal of his prey.

In that instant, as the agony of death pierced the air and the pride of a successful hunt shook me, I was more wolf than man, and the danger began to grow more imminent.

I stepped next to him and snuffled at his catch, watched him rend the flesh. Blood fountained up as an artery was struck, spurted crimson across his dark snout, stained his teeth, dotted the snow around us. It steamed in the cold air, this blood, and it had a smell uniquely its own.

I howled.

We tore at the animal together, and he kept his eyes on me for a long while, cold gray eyes that did not disclose the thoughts behind them. When we were done, our noses red and the snow around us sodden, I did not feel disgusted, but rather invigorated.

We turned back to our original pursuit and gained the shifting walls of mists through which I would have to pass.

"I want to return," I growled.

"So?" His breath reeked.

"May I return?"

"For what purpose?"

"To join your pack."

"That is most unwise. That is foolish, and you know it, and you must journey. Be gone."

Then he turned and loped away, head hunched between his rugged shoulders, eating up yards in a single bounding leap.

Looking up at the even gray of the sky, I felt a hollow longing within me, and I pawed the snow away from the earth, dug the ground into a crosshatch of runnels. I wiped my bloodied snout in the snow and lapped the stained whiteness. I wanted to remain here forever, without regard to my true heritage and nature, to bound after the disappearing wolf and follow him to his pack. In the night hours, there would be deep dens in hidden caves to sleep in warmth and to climb upon some sleek and lovely female with gray eyes and a shiny black snout. During the daylight hours, there would be prowling in the fields and in the sparsely treed grounds before the thickness of the forests themselves. There would be blood and camaraderie, running together, killing together, defying the leaden skies with my fellows....

Yet there was some nagging reason why I should go beyond the mists to the next segment of this landscape, though I could not remember what it was. I stepped through the mists, tensed, but found no danger, only cool wetness. I growled deep in my throat and broke through to the other side.

The journey continued.

In the new section of the subconscious universe, there was a taste of Ireland: stony ground, rolling hills so low that one could be seen beyond the other, the smell of the sea, flat areas of land marshy with the backwash of the tidelands. Waiting for me by a column of limestone that stood like a proscenium pillar without benefit of its stage, was a centaur. His head was ringed with golden curls which fell to his shoulders and framed a face of striking masculinity: broad forehead above deep black eyes that spoke of perserverance and a strong will, high aristocratic cheekbones, a proud Roman nose, a blocky chin. His shoulders were brawny, his arms rippling with muscles that seemed to possess a will and intent of their own. From the middle of his flat belly on down, he was a black stallion of formidable proportions, the lines of a thoroughbred in his long legs.

"My name is Kasostrous, and you may call me Kas," he said.

"Call me Simeon," I growled, my voice a tangled hiss of barely understandable guttural syllables.

"You must now acquire the form of the centaur," Kas said, leaving the limestone thrust and ambling toward me. His hooves clacked on the stony ground, sent sparks up once or twice. His long, flashing length of tail whipped in the breeze, tossed from side to side with lazy power.

"I like wolfhood," I said, pawing the ground, my nails whispering on the dew-damp rock. I continued to stroke, sharpening them for later kills.

"You like it too well," Kas said. "That is the trouble."

"What's that supposed to mean?" I asked, staring up at him wtih my flint eyes, hoping to strike terror in him. I failed.

"You have fallen into the danger of identifying too closely with the analogue you permit your psychic energy to assume. Though such energy is malleable, the surface tension can grow stronger with time, sap the will to return to any other analogue, any other shape. Too long a time as a wolf, and you will find yourself trapped not only in the form, but in the character of the creature."

"Nonsense." But the word was said without conviction and in such a guttural rumble that it only reinforced what Kas said.

"You disprove your own words."

"I'm an esper," I said.

"So?"

"I understand these things."

"You do not grasp the difference of this subconscious

universe," he said. "There is a certain thing about it which will trap you—you especially, given your past and your mental condition."

I pawed the earth. "Help me grasp it," I said at last, doubtful. I did not want to have to believe what he was saying. I only wanted to be free to run and tear flesh and mount the sleek females in the dark shadows of the dens.

"Child's mental landscape is peopled only with creatures from legends and mythology. He read extensively in those areas from the moment he could understand language, and he viewed hundreds of senso-tapes on the subject. It interested him, because he thought he might find a purpose even stronger than the one which was connected with the Christian mythos: the Second Coming which he believed was himself."

"But this wolf does not take the form of a mythological creature," I argued with my wolf-mouth.

"There is a Tibetan legend which tells of monks transformed to wolves. They were men who loved luxury and betrayed the true intentions of their religion. They indulged in women and in drink, in jewels and in food, and all that was pretty and satisfying to the senses. Their god came to them after they had defiled mere children in a brothel contaminated with all manners of evil. In the disguise of demons, their god offered them immortality for their souls. It was a test to see if they were completely depraved, or whether there was still some minim of decency within them. But all nine of the monks eagerly grasped the straw of endless life at the sacrifice of nirvana, of eternal life on another plane. And so he gave them immortality and crushed their souls. But he gave them immortality as wolves, as vicious reeking creatures hated and feared by all, creatures who could no longer know a woman's form but must run in dank dens, creatures unable to make or appreciate the taste of wine or of a succulently prepared roast."

"And you want me now to be a centaur."

"Yes. The oftener you change, the less chance you have to be absorbed by any one particular mythical prototype. And you, seeking some purpose beyond your human one, are ripe for such an end as threatens you now."

"I can withstand the pressure."

"You can't," Kas said. He shook golden curls out of his eyes. "You especially. All your life, just like Child, you have relied heavily upon a mythological ill-logic to justify your existence."

"Christian mythos," I corrected, wondering why I was still trying to defend it.

"These are of the same level of value as the Christian one. One will snare you as easily as the other. In all of them, you will find the same simplicity and attractive lack of complication as you found in Christianity's legends. And you will never leave this place."

I thought, for the first time, of Melinda. I had been forcing her and everything else out of my mind, refusing to acknowledge her no-nonsense interviews in that other world, her quick wit, and her supple and willing body. Now they all rose and crowded into my consciousness at the same moment, almost overwhelming me.

In time, as we stood there on the rolling earth under the flat sky, listening to the sea, Kas said, "Will you?"

"What?"

"Change?"

"I guess . . . guess so."

"Soon, then."

I hesitated.

"Soon."

And I changed.

Together, we started off across the hilly land, galloping under the steel blue of looming thunderhead clouds. My own golden hair streamed behind me. My tail rode straight out behind, fluttering in the fingers of the sea-tinged air.

If anything, this was better than the form of a wolf, carried more of a sense of freedom and delight.

Child was not to be found here, either. We searched everywhere, including the flat white beach where the surf curled. We trotted through the shushing foam of the sea, kicking up shells and sending crabs in frantic flight. We left our hoofprints in the sucking mud of the moors, in the rich black earth of the grasslands, in the sand by the ocean. Sure-footed, we climbed the few small peaks and surveyed this sector of the world, looked for caves and came back down again. In time, when it was apparent there was no blue-floored room and no exit to Child's conscious mind, we reached the curtain of mist to another climate, another segment of the fractured reality that constituted Child's mind.

I was forced to say goodbye to Kas the centaur, though I longed to stay here and enjoy the horseman form a while longer. He lectured me about disassociating from my centaur form upon leaving this plane, and I listened and made my promises.

In the next landscape, I returned to my human analogue, though shedding the horseman form was painful and filled me with a sad need to feel my hooves striking stone. There was no life here to imitate, so I did not have to worry about becoming inextricably meshed with a myth figure. This was the land of the broken black mountains which jagged up in slabs as big as houses, some even larger than that, like a world of broken crockery and shattered bottles. The sunlight was discolored by the refracting stone and became a depressing brown. The air was flat, as if it had been bottled for a long while, and no breeze moved in it. There were no sounds, no movements. The sky was an even, ugly yellow, like dark mustard, and not a single cloud marked its expanse.

I walked forward.

The onyx rocks were smooth and cold against my bare feet.

As I scrabbled up the terrain, my fingers squeaked on the shiny surfaces. Those sounds seemed unendurably long in the ghostly silence. I did not like this place at all, wanted out of it as fast as I could move to the next veil of mist. But it was here that I found Child, found the place where he was trapped in his own madness....

IV

As I made my way over the ebony land, I reached a chasm in the shattered rocks, perhaps a thousand yards long and three yards wide at the top, narrowing to two feet at the bottom. Down there, some three hundred feet below, a soft blue light glowed. It seemed to be the gentle blue of shallow water, but even this slight color branded my eyes in contrast to the sameness of the terrain I had been struggling across for some minutes.

I called down, listened to the flat echo, but received no answer. If this was the place where Child waited, bound by his own insanity, circled by unnamed demons, he was unable to speak.

I swung over the jagged edge, looked to the bottom, then grew wings like those I had seen on the batlike creatures of the mountain. I descended gently, pulled the wings in and absorbed them as the way grew too narrow to glide. I dropped the last few feet onto the blue floor, found it was made of ice.

To the right, the rock wall cut off three feet above the ice, and the passage this created seemed to go on for some distance. Lying on my stomach, I slid along the shimmering ice; I was cold but not uncomfortable, exhilarated by the freshness of the air here. A hundred feet further on, the ceiling of black rock thrust suddenly upward, and I found myself in a full-sized cavern where I could stand.

On my feet again, I crossed the barren room to the far side where the ice-encrusted rock seemed to warp downward. There, I discovered steps roughly chiseled in the ice. I went down them, cautiously, eventually came out in a shadowy chamber with another blue floor, though this one was not empty: Child sat in the center of it in an analogue version of his real body.

And . . .

And: the things crawled around him, circling in mindlessness, yet with a certain uncompromising evil that terrified me even though I knew they could not do me any physical harm. They were much like scorpions though somewhat longer than a man's arm, with flared, knife-edged carapaces shielding their backs, and twenty spindly legs on either side. Their stinging tails forked at the end, each of the two prongs tipped with a trio of wicked spurs as long as my little finger and tapered to needle points. They did not look at me, nor did their sensory cilia, bursting like whiskers around their beaked mouths, in any way indicate that they realized my presence.

Their legs hissed on the ice, and their constant parade had worn shallow grooves in the cold floor.

There were different numbers of them at different moments. Now there might be as few as a dozen describing the wide circle—now a hundred of them, magically crystallizing out of the crisp air—now thirty, now a dozen, now two dozen. No matter how hard I looked, I could not catch one of them appearing or disappearing, though their numbers fluctuated with every passing second. I had the feeling that I was in a funhouse where there was a complicated array of trick mirrors and that there was actually but one of these creatures whose presence was magnified to one degree or another by ingenious, mirrored pyrotechnics.

"Child?" I called.

The withered dwarf paid no attention to me, but stared with morbid fascination at the nightmarish scorpion guards which kept him ringed in and obedient.

Since I had first been trapped in this subconscious reality, I had not spared the time or the energy to consider the reason and psychology behind many of the mental analogues that constituted this inner universe. I had merely accepted and tried to deal with them, to search through them for a way out, a way to freedom and my own body. Now, as I watched the grisly parade before me, I began to wonder what this collection of monsters was representative of. Why was Child's core of energy and intelligence trapped in this place, bound to this single minim of his entire subconscious universe? What were these scorpions that surrounded him and maintained their constant, evil vigil?

I examined them more closely and discovered that they did not have that surface sheen of reality that the centaur and the wolf had possessed. They shifted, as if they were liquid, and fragments of thought associations whirled inside of them. It took only a moment to discover their true nature.

Consider the human mind: three main parts to it: the ego, the superego, and the id. The first is what we are and what we have reached through the ordeals of life; the second is what we think we are and what we attempt to delude others into considering us as; the third is all the things we want to be and do but which—either because of public condemnation or a conflict with our own superegos and guilt—we never dare consider. In the id, there are the dark facets of our human soul, pieces of racial heritage and other parts uniquely ours: blood lust and the desire to rend flesh; sexual longings of grotesque sorts and on grotesque scales; the urge to cannibalism, the hunger for the taste of human meat. We repress the id and most of us do not even realize that it stirs within us like a worm in the apple, so complete is our veil of civilization.

These scorpion-tailed monstrosities were Child's id lusts, his ugly needs which he, like everyone, had always kept repressed. It was impossible to say how they had gotten free, how they had encircled him like this, but I ventured a guess or two as I watched them clack horny mandibles and lift rattling, bony legs. Perhaps, when he had considered himself the Second Coming, he had been unable to pretend the id lusts did not exist. Perhaps, finally, in order to continue thinking of himself as a deity, he had to rip the id from the other parts of his mind, tear it free of the ego and the superego. And now those lusts were attempting to integrate themselves with his mind, to establish contact with the ethereal fragments of his thought processes, where they belonged. Or perhaps the id had been broken loose of the rest of his mind when he had tipped into insanity. Either way, they had found him again, and they had spell-bound him with their evil. He held them off with his psychic energy, still unable to tolerate their being a part of him. (Did he still nurture the Second-Coming fantasy—or perhaps some equal legend from another mythology?)

"Child?" I asked again.

Again: no answer.

If I could free him, if only for a moment, could contact him and jar him into a moment of sanity, perhaps I could get him to open a way into his conscious mind, a path to lead me out of his body. But as long as the scorpions were there, as long as he was transfixed by the sight of these lusts he had forgotten, I could not reach him.

For the third time since I had first entered his mind that day so long ago, I fashioned a sword from the air, a shimmering blue luminosity with a curving blade and a hilt of dazzling light. Stepping forward, I hacked at the first of the scorpions in my way, halved it. It vanished. I turned to a second of them, tore it through, then swung furiously, wading through the spinning members of the huge creatures, destroying them as fast as the magic mirrors brought them to my attention.

Their sound was a screeching cacophony, and their mandibles punctuated the wailing fury with a drumbeat of irregular snapping, thrumming clacks against the ice floor.

I do not know how long the battle lasted. It seemed

that perhaps days passed, though there was no sunrise and sunset down there—and I did not tire in my analogue body, did not need to stop for food and drink. I was the irresistible force, wading into the legs and tails and shining carapaces. In time, the numbers of the scorpions began to grow smaller, and at last the air refused to disgorge more of them. I knew they were not gone forever, because they were nothing more than psychic energy, and that could never be truly destroyed. But by then, I would not care if they encircled him.

Child still sat on the ice, staring where the scorpions had marched but where there was now nothing but scored ice. Approaching his analogue cautiously, I touched him, hunkered before him.

"Child?"

Quiet.

"Child? Speak to me?"

He looked at me. He blinked his eyes. And then chaos broke loose as his insanity boiled through the surface tension of the analogue and swept over me!

I was swept up, up, on a tide of human flesh, of torn arms and legs, of bleeding mouths, broken teeth, shattered bones, burning flesh, splintered eyeballs. Monsters rose in the swell and came toward me, lumbering ogres and swimming reptilian horrors. The arms and mouths in the ocean of human parts attacked me, grasped me and tried to pull me down, bit me and chewed at my unreal psychic flesh.

I felt myself losing hold of my own equilibrium. In a moment, I would spiral over the edge, into madness for the second time. I had recovered only recently, and I knew a second plunge to the bottom of that well would be the last I would ever make. I would fall back into gibbering incoherency, and I would remain there forever. Twice mad is once too often, and the shores of detached logic would never be available to me again.

The nearest ogre reached for me, with his seven-fingered hands, each finger tipped with the fanged mouth of a yellow-eyed snake.

I rolled across the rippling floor of human parts, kicking pieces of bodies up as I went.

The snake fingers missed by inches.

A flurry of mutilated corpses clutched me and pulled me under the surface of the sea.

I fought to air again, through nightmare conglomerations of dead men and women.

"CHILD!" I screamed.

Another ogre thundered down on me.

In the last moment before I could be grasped and dismembered, I did the only thing that would save me. Giving myself over to the basest of my id lusts, radiating bloodhunger and sexual need of the vilest sort, I repelled the ogres and the dragons, forced back the tide of human bodies that tore at me. In seconds, I was back on the blue ice floor where again the analogue of Child sat, tranced.

I circled him. Now I was in the form of one of the great scorpion beasts, mandibles chattering, forked stinging tail raised above my back, ready to attack.

His psychic energy formed a wall against me, but I danced on, broached that wall with my own mind, and leaped upon him, thrashing with him on the floor. This time, rather than argue with him, rather than plead with him, I devoured his psychic energy, destroyed him, absorbed him, and dissipated his shattered mind throughout my own.

Child no longer existed. I had killed him. But now I was in total control of his body. I left that place, made it dissolve around me. I made the mountain appear, and I climbed it, entered the caves through which I had first come down into Child's subconscious mind. In moments, I had freed myself, and was looking out at the world through Child's eyes, encased, again, in real flesh. . . .

THREE

The Incomplete Creation...

I

I found myself in Child's body, lying in a hospital bed with the barred sides raised to provide the illusion of a prison. The room was a private one, somewhere far up in the tower of Artificial Creation, no doubt. There was no light but that from a small blue bulb plugged directly into a floor socket. In that eerie glow, I could see that there was no nurse in attendance. How long had Child lain like this, dazed, almost comatose, unable to speak or see or hear anything of the real world as his madness kept him sealed in the analogue of his subconscious? Days or weeks? Perhaps even years?

Somewhat frantic at that last thought, I pushed up, weak and dizzy. My frail, bony arms felt as if they would crack, but they got me to the edge of the bed just the same. My short legs dangled a foot from the tiles after I got the barred slats down, and that measly twelve inches looked more like two or three miles. I built my courage, dropped, felt skinny legs buckle. I crashed forward on my face and lay there for a while, collecting my wits.

Was this what it was like for Child, this inability to cope with the inadequacies of his own body, this helplessness and dependence? No wonder his own search for a purpose and identity had been so much more thorough and extensive than my own.

I got on hands and knees and gripped the edge of the bed for support, gained my feet again. The door was but a dozen steps away. I toddled toward it, collapsed against it, holding on to the knob to keep from taking another serious fall.

Opening the door was a major chore, compounded by the fact that I wanted to do it quietly. I didn't want anyone to know that I was awake now and moving around. First, I wanted to find out a few things, attempt to discover how long I had been trapped in Child's mind. And if I could somehow locate my own body—for, surely, they were keeping it somewhere close at hand, in another dark hospital room—and re-enter it before they were aware I had returned, I would be in a better position to take care of myself. I didn't trust Morsfagen or any other super-patriot professional soldier. The more ignorant I was about what had transpired since I had gone mad within Child, the further removed I was from my own body and, therefore, autonomy, the more power they would hold over me, the more they could demand and perpetrate.

The door finally opened and gave a view of an empty corridor that was painted a flat, unreflective blue. I stepped out of the room, closed the door, and hung by the wall, breathing heavily and trying to ignore the pain in the sunken chest of the mutant body which I inhabited.

I didn't care if I destroyed Child's body during this trek, for I had already destroyed Child himself by absorbing his psychic energy back there in that blue-floored room beneath the broken, ebony plain. He would never own his body again. I could feel his intellect, devoid of any personality now, within my own mind, magnifying my intelligence and perceptions. But that was the only minim of Child's real self that would ever survive.

Pushing away from the wall, I started down the corridor. I could not expect it to remain empty for long, and I would gain nothing by being seen here, before I had learned anything of my situation. I weaved from wall to wall, barely managing to keep my feet. And when the tall, uniformed man appeared at the head of the stairwell and shouted in surprise, I collapsed on my face....

When I woke, I was in the same hospital room, in the same bed, with the metal slats raised around the sides to keep me from falling out. There were differences, though. There was plenty of light, and there was a nurse, a buxom, gray-haired matron with a bland, pleasant face and a concerned look plastered all over it. There was a guard by the door, on the inside, his holster unsnapped. Why I should be considered that much of a threat when I could hardly even walk, I did not know. Morsfagen and a white-smocked physician stood by the right side of my bed, looking down at me. The physician exhibited concern and professional interest. Morsfagen had a look of hatred and sheer animal cunning.

"Welcome back," he said.

"I'm thirsty," I croaked, realizing for the first time how parched my throat was.

The nurse brought me water, which I gulped eagerly. The chips of ice rattled against my teeth, stung my gums. But it was all quite good, better than expensive wine.

"No more water, no more anything until some questions are answered," the general said.

"Yes," I replied.

"What has happened to Simeon Kelly?"

For a moment, I was surprised. Then I realized that they had no way of knowing this wasn't Child who had awakened. It meant that there were other things they could not know, things which would give me the upper hand.

"I am Kelly," I said.

"No games," he snapped.

"This isn't."

He looked at me closely. "Maybe you had better explain."

So I told him about Child's investigation into the nature of God. He did not seem moved by the discovery that the universe held no purpose, that God is insane and always has been. Perhaps he did not believe me. I rather think that was the case with the doctor and the nurse and the guard by the door. But there was a crisp, cold gaze there that said Morsfagen did believe—and not only that he believed, but that he had come to the same conclusions himself some time ago, though he had simply lacked the proof that Child had managed to obtain. There was no room for God in Morsfagen's life, I realized. He had always operated outside a belief in heaven and hell and retribution for sin.

I carefully avoided mentioning that I had absorbed Child's energy, that he would never regain his body. If they thought that all could soon be returned to normal, they would be more eager to see me back in my own flesh, wherever it was kept.

When I was done, I asked: "How much time has passed?"

"A month," he said.

It was startling, yet it could have been worse. I had steeled myself to accept the word "years," and this was a blessing by comparison. A lot could have happened in a month. But Melinda might still be free, might still be waiting. Harry would be alive. My house would not have been sold to creditors. Yes, there was still time to regain normality.

"I want my own body," I said. That was the first step to that normality.

"Perhaps," Morsfagen said.

I looked around at the others to see whether they understood the cruelty in that tease. None of them seemed to pay any attention. Perhaps part of their jobs included paying no attention to such things.

"What is this—perhaps?" I asked.

Child's voice box made the words seem sinister when they were actually spoken in fear.

"Perhaps," he said, his face impassive, "it would be better for all of us if no one outside of this room ever discovered that you have regained sanity and are ready to return to your own body. It would be less trouble to get you doing work for us. We would not have to pay you anything. All in all, perhaps it would be a wise idea."

The nurse paid no attention. But her pleasant face mirrored her tacit agreement with Morsfagen.

The doctor took my pulse, listened at my chest with a stethoscope, checked my eyes and ears, ignoring what transpired around him.

The guard, by the door, had Morsfagen's impassive look.

I was alone.

Except for Child's intellect, which had expanded my own. There was a cunning about me now that I had not possessed before. Morsfagen would think he knew me: fast on the cutting remarks, but low on cleverness. But that had changed, and I was now every bit as devious as he.

"One problem," I said.

"What's that?"

"I've told you that it took me this full month to shake loose of my own madness and to free myself from Child's insanity. I nearly lost my mind again trying to find a way through his subconscious landscape. You scanning all this so far?" He indicated that he was by saying nothing. "Now, if I'm trapped in this frame, welded so closely to his mind, I'm going to succumb to his insanity again—and this time it will be permanent. I couldn't stand the ordeal of recovery again." In that whispered, deathlike rattle of Child's, the words took on even more sincerity than I had tried to give them.

Morsfagen looked doubtful. It was almost as if he could sense the change in me, sense the expanded awareness and cunning. But he could not take the chance that I was not telling him the truth, and he knew that I had won. He was going to have to console himself with the fact that at least he now had me in full mind for future use; if he tried to play for full stakes and keep me locked in Child's body, he might very well wind up with nothing. And military careers are not built on blunders.

"Bring him along," he ordered the doctor. "We'll let him have his body back." He smiled at me, but it was not a pleasant smile. "But you'd better cooperate, Kelly. It's time of war now, and that rules out your brand of frivolity."

"I understand perfectly," I said, not without a touch of sarcasm.

"I'm sure you do."

And he left the room.

Minutes later, they wheeled me into the corridor to keep my rendezvous with my own coma-ridden flesh. . . .

All the while, I gloried in the thought that I was swiftly getting the upper hand and that before they realized what had happened, I would be in my former position of dominance. There were two minds' worth of energy within me, plus the complex intellect of Child now amplifying my own. They were mere men, I told myself, and they stood no chance at all.

I did not realize that I was making the same mistake that I had made twice before. In the old days, I had convinced myself that I was a god of sorts, the Second Coming, and my life had been disastrous because of that fantasy. In Child's subconscious, I had eagerly sought to be transformed into the mythic images of Tibetan wolves, into something transcending humanity, and that might have cost me my mind and my eventual recovery. And now, as I was wheeled down the corridor, I again looked at myself as more than a man, as a minor god soon to prove his power. Because I had never allowed myself to associate with "mere men," I did not understand them, or myself. And my latest delusions of grandeur were bound to lead to ultimate disaster....

And did...

II

My legs were cramped, and even a slight bit of movement made my shoulders ache, for the staff had not been exercising my body with the proper degree of enthusiasm during the month it had been vacant. I felt weak, and my stomach was a hard knot. Having been fed intravenously for some four weeks, the stomach had shrunk and felt like a clenched fist in there, squeezing my guts. Otherwise: fine. And since it was such a delight to be housed in my own flesh once again, I was willing to overlook the little aches and pains of readjustment to life. I didn't complain, and I tried not even to grimace.

Morsfagen seemed disappointed by that.

They wheeled Child's carcass out of the room. It would continue to live, though it would never exhibit intelligence again. It was a husk, nothing more. I still had not told them, for I was still not free of the AC complex and out of their immediate reach. Morsfagen would not take kindly to such a trick, and I didn't want to be around whenever he discovered it.

I showered, washed away the weeks of sickbed smell. The hot water seemed to loosen my cramped muscles, and dressing was only half the ordeal I had expected. When I slipped into my jacket and checked my reflection in the mirror, Morsfagen said, "Your shyster is waiting downstairs."

I held back the witty reply designed to demolish him, for I knew that was exactly what he wanted. He was searching for some reason to slap me down, either with his fists or with a preventive detention arrest. Why we had hit it off so miserably from the start, and why our hatred for each other was now twice what it had been, I didn't know. True, we were altogether different types, but the antagonism we felt for each other was deeper and more unremitting than a mere clash of personalities.

"Thank you," I said, leaving him with nothing to attack. I walked to the door, opened it, and was halfway into the corridor before he replied.

"You're welcome."

I turned and looked at him and saw that he was smiling, that same cold smile of hatred which I had grown used to by then. He had said "you're welcome," but not with any seriousness—which meant that he understood me and knew that I understood him too.

"We'll contact you day after tomorrow," he said. "There's a lot of work to do. But, after what you've been through, you deserve a little rest."

"Thank you," I said.

"You're welcome."

Again. And grinning this time too...

I closed the door and walked down the hall to the bank of elevators with a dark-haired, blue-eyed, six-foot-four-inch guard as company. We didn't say much of anything to each other on our way downstairs, not so much out of any particular dislike for each other as out of a sheer lack of anything to say, like a nuclear physicist and an uneducated carpenter at the same cocktail party, neither exactly superior, but both separated by a mammoth communications gap.

Down...

Harry was in the lobby, tearing his hat apart, and when the elevator doors opened, he gave the thing a particularly vicious mangling with his big hands and started toward us. He was smiling the first genuine, friendly, uncomplicated smile I had seen since I had awakened in Child's body. He hugged me, living up to the image of the father figure, and he had tears in his eyes which he could not manage to conceal.

I was not concealing my own tears at all. I dearly loved this clumsy, pudgy, sloppily dressed Irishman, though most of my life had been spent in playing down that love. Maybe it was because I had learned early to hate and despise as self-protection. When Harry separated me from that world inside the AC complex and showed me what actual love was, I never lost my suspicion. And it is easier to act less involved so that if you're hurt later, the anguish doesn't show so much and give your adversary satisfaction. Now unchecked, evidence of that love flowed.

We hurried across the lobby to the second elevator bank and went down to the underground garage, where the attendant brought Harry's hovercar, accepted a tip, and stepped back as we drove out of that great, sparkling building. In the street, we both sighed, as if some weight had been lifted from us, and we began to talk for the first time, out of the range of those microphones which infest any government building.

"You'll tell me about it now," he said, his eyes flicking from the shifting layers of new snow on the street to where I sat against the far door. "They wouldn't let me up to see you but once a week, you know."

"You'd only have been looking at flesh and blood," I said. "All this time, I've been inside of Child, locked down there in his mind."

"As I figured," he said. "But those"—he jerked his thumb behind us, twisting his face up to look disgusted—"those pretty boys in their uniforms, I just don't trust."

"They didn't exercise my body properly. And they didn't take any precautions against stomach shrinkage. Otherwise, I'm fine."

He snorted. "So tell me."

"You first. I've spent a month in that place, and I don't have the foggiest notion what has happened out here. When I went in, war had all but been declared. The Chinese and the Japanese had crossed the Soviet border, maybe nuked a town. . . ."

He looked grim, stared at the street unfolding before us for a long time before he said anything. It was dark, and the crisp blue arc lights sent fantastic shadows wriggling between the heavy fall of snowflakes. The streets seemed almost empty of traffic.

"War was declared two days later," he said.

"And we won?"

"Partly."

I looked around at the streets, all undamaged, all occupied by our own troops, our own police. Indeed, I saw now that the amount of occupation of our territory spelled some sort of trouble. Every other street corner contained coppers parked in squad-carrying howlers, surveying the dark boulevard. They watched us go by with quick, dark glances, though they offered no pursuit.

"Partly?" I asked.

As we flitted across the city, he summed up the developments of the month-long war:

The Chinese had indeed nuked Zavitaya, for there was nothing there any longer but powdered stone, splintered wood, and the ruins of a very few outlying structures. Of the moderately large population, there were six hundred survivors.

Belogorsk was taken, its laboratories seized and impressed into the service of the People's Army of China—a euphemism for the military strong-arm of the Peking dictatorship and its Japanese allies. Within a day, hover-trucks had taxied Chinese troops into Svobodnyy and Shimanovsk, thereby effectively isolating one small sector of the Soviet Union.

In this time, the Western Alliance had been making preparations and issuing stern warnings to the Chinese, who had ignored them imperiously, sparing no effort to make it apparent that they considered the West with scorn. The United Nations was petitioned by every Western Alliance nation, and the world organization replied by trade sanctions against China. These too were laughed off. The land of the dragon was feeling its muscle for the first time in many centuries, and its egotism threatened to carry it to the brink of world destruction and beyond. Yet the Alliance held off, well aware that the electronic shield envisioned by Child and later torn from his mind by my own extrasensory powers was reaching midpoint in its hasty construction. There was no sense, the strategists agreed, in helping to escalate a mini-war into a major conflagration until our side was immune to attack behind its shield generators and victory was assured the West.

Two weeks after the start of the war, the Chinese were still consolidating territorial gains, moving more troops into the captured Russian territory. All the while, they pointed to their Dragonfly and made lightly veiled threats. They made false promises that this was all the land they wanted. And they followed such worthless assurances with warnings that they could easily survive a nuclear-bacteriological war, for their population was so much greater than ours that it could not help but outlast us.

The Alliance, furious, bided time.

Then, unexpectedly, Japanese forces had landed on Formosa, coming in from the sea with destroyers and landing craft. While the guns and the forces were aimed at China, the back door was entered and the house secured by the enemy. The Alliance forces quartered on that strategic airbase were systematically slaughtered. Both the Chinese and the Japanese denied having anything to do with it. But reconnaissance planes reported Japanese ships, sans the rising sun, harbored in the islands.

The following day, with even the peace criers united behind the government, the crash force working to erect electronic shields over all the strategic areas of the Western Alliance, the last of the invisible shells of stretched molecules in place and the generators backed with a second set to prevent disaster, the Alliance declared war on China and Japan.

We struck out with nuclear stockpiles at the major industrial centers of both enemy nations. In hours, billions in property and hundreds of thousands of lives were wiped out in gushes of mile-high flame. The enemy was prepared for this, and it retaliated with its own nuclear weaponry. But the shields worked, the Alliance cities remained intact. Again and again, the People's Army rained missiles upon points in Russia, Europe, and North America. Not one of them did damage. Since all sides had long ago, for obvious strategic reasons concerned with occupying captured territory, gone to the construction of "clean" bombs, even the spill radiation did not kill people living in the countryside beyond the shelter of the unseen domes of molecules which had been stretched to stunningly large dimensions, their surface tension curiously increased and not decreased by that expansion.

In desperation, plague drops were made on the cities of the Alliance, but even these did not penetrate. In the countryside, people died, but even many of these were saved by immunization teams from the cities. Property damage, at this point, was zero.

The Chinese nuked the small, unprotected towns in a final spasm of fury, but they had little firepower left.

The Japanese had already surrendered in order to protect what little unmolested lands the home islands still contained.

The Chinese command center was discovered at last, destroyed with a vengeance, and the war brought to and end. Or so everyone thought....

"Thought?" I asked.

"We have ambitious men for our military leaders," Harry explained. His tone was none too pleasant.

"Go on."

"We made a mistake with the voluntary, reformed military service laws," he said.

"How so?"

"Try to envision these men, Sim. They're well-paid professionals. There hasn't been a draft within the Alliance for twenty-four years. They enlist because they like to be a part of a protective Big Brother sort of organization —and because combat and planning for combat excites them. We turned ourselves over to those who enjoy war, and we gave them the machines to wage it. Now, with all this hardware and all this education in the ways of dealing death, they had had to sit through fourteen years of cold war where guns were never fired. And before that, there were two decades of total peace, where nations hardly even exchanged angry words. They've never had the chance to prove themselves, and since they are basically the sort of men who need to prove themselves for their own benefit, they've been driven up the wall by brinksmanship and peace."

I felt ill, without exactly understanding why. The night seemed darker and colder, and I had a sudden and furious need for Melinda, for the touch of her and the warmth, the seeking together and the final closeness. It was such an intense desire that I grew dizzy with it.

"So?" I managed to ask.

"So, they didn't want to stop. They were moving, living their dreams, and loving it. They were on the edge of the thing they'd all fantasized about—conquering the world. They could incorporate every nation into the Alliance, and then it would be over. All the plans and subplans, plots and counterplots and counter-counterplots came together in a marvelous mosaic, and they just couldn't resist. China was occupied, but the artillery was turned, next, on South America."

"They're neutral!"

"Mostly," he agreed. "But the Alliance generals were bothered by South America's autonomy, especially since Brazil had been making that space effort of theirs pay off with the mineral ships from Titan. The continent fell in slightly less than a week—yesterday, to be exact. They were either badly prepared militarily, or had oriented their armies toward the exploration of space. They've come under the banner of the Alliance—angrily, reluctantly, but under it."

"And all the countries already in the Alliance—they all went along with this?"

"Not all. But in Russia, the military had taken control of the government years before. France and Italy knuckled under to the popular sentiment of their people, of the common man. Spain is a military nation to start with—no problem there."

"But Britain and the U.S. wouldn't stand for it!" It sounded false.

"Britain did refuse, said she wouldn't supply her own men for the Alliance endeavor. But she gave tacit approval by continuing trade and diplomatic relationships with all her allies. She's too small to really buck them, and she could only maintain her military's integrity, nothing more. Canada did the same, though Quebec declared independence and won it—or at least had the last time I heard—and joined the militant ranks of the other Alliance nations. As for us, the U.S., we were in it from the moment the Soviet generals made the suggestion. The peace criers were right all along: a volunteer army can become a secondary government and can threaten the elected one if the time is ripe. The coup came two mornings after the Soviet proposal when it became obvious that the elected government was not going to agree to a world-wide campaign. We are now ruled by a police-army coalition, by a council of eighteen generals and admirals, and the war—meantime—goes on."

"Who now?"

"Australia," he said. "She has become self-sufficient, which the Alliance military advisors never have appreciated. Sydney was obliterated this afternoon and an ultimatum was delivered to the Australian government shortly thereafter."

Neither of us spoke for a while.

The snow continued to fall, faster than ever.

"Dictatorship then?" I asked.

"They won't call it that."

"Nazism?"

"It's a mistake to apply the terms of other eras. The same sense of chauvinism is there, and a roiling muck of nationalistic fantasies. You can bet the Alliance factions will break down in a monumental squabble once this war is over. The Russians against us, a real Armageddon. They have the taste of blood, and the old hates have been resurrected on all sides."

"And nothing can be done?"

He didn't answer me, aware that it was an unanswerable question. He just drove and looked morose and contributed to my flagging spirits.

This was the age of instant history. More could happen in a week than happened in a year in the previous century. Everything moved, relentlessly, determinedly, and we were all caught up by it, swept along, either to be drowned in the swell or carried to a foreign shore on the wave crests.

I had a feeling I was going to be one of those to drown. I was valuable to the war machinery. And even when the war was over, I could serve the junta with my esp, help to oppress those at home who would not appreciate the beauty of a military nation. And I didn't know whether I could do that, for I might be one of those rebelling myself. All my life I had been floundering from one emotional disaster to another, drawing in and in and in upon myself. And then I had met Melinda, had been treated by my Porter-Rainey Solid-State headshrinker, and had opened myself to the world for the first time, had tasted pure freedom and enjoyed it. The loss of my sanity within Child's mind and the long attempt to get free of him had interrupted my enjoyment of that new-found peace. And now that I was back, now that Melinda and a pleasant future lay within my grasp, the world was in the hands of the madmen who threatened to tear it apart.

But I couldn't drown. I had to ride those wave crests, had to survive to keep Melinda surviving. Damn them and their bombs and their war lusts!

As we drove, I felt my rage grow, swell, encompass my entire mind. And I realized that it would not be good enough to ride those crests. At most, the two of us would come out alive, washed ashore after the apocalypse, with each other. But our world would be destroyed and useless, and we would have no freedom, then, at all. Life would be a constant battle for survival in a society thrown back to barbarism. No, what I was going to have to do was forget about riding the crests of the waves—and find some way to direct the tides of the entire damn ocean of our future!

"Not that I don't find your company perfectly marvelous," I told Harry, "but could you take me to Melinda's place instead of yours?"

He hesitated before he said it, but he said it just the same. "She isn't at her place, Sim. She's been arrested. She's a political prisoner."

It took long seconds for the words to sink in. When they did, my rage became godly wrath, and I began to seek someone upon whom to vent it. I was not afraid for her safety. I basked in the certainty of my power. I still did not see that I was bound up in the same flawed philosophy that had brought me to ruin so many times before. . . .

III

I stood by the window of Harry's den, holding a glass of brandy which I had not yet tasted. Beyond the window: a copse of trees, snow-covered grass, white-bearded hedgerows. The stark, wintry vista matched my thoughts, as I considered what Harry had told me on the way over. Melinda had become engaged in writing pamphlets for some revolutionary group and had been under surveillance. Upon the magazine publication of the first part of her biography of my life—the childhood years in the AC complex—she had been arrested for questioning in connection with the death of a copper and the destruction of a howler some two weeks before. Whether there had been any questioning or not, no one would know; she was still under arrest.

The magazine article had not merely been a biography, but had contained scorchingly anti-military, anti-AC anecdotes which neither of us had decided, before my entombment in Child's mind, whether we should risk using or not. She had risked it.

"When is the trial?" I asked him now. We had postponed further discussion until we were warm and comfortable in his den—at his insistence.

"A date has been docketed before the Military Court of Emergency. Next September."

"Seven and a half months!" I turned from the window, furious, slopping brandy over my wrist.

"When the act is labeled treason, there are laws that permit it."

"What's her bail?" I asked.

"There is none."

"Is none?"

"What I said."

"But the law allows——"

He held up his pudgy hand to stop me. He looked terrible, as if telling me this was worse on him than on me. "This is no longer a republic, remember. It is a military state where men like the junta councilmen decide what laws there shall be. For sedition, they now say, there is no bail, and the rule of preventive detention has been extended indefinitely."

"Fight them!" I bellowed. "You fought them for me when——"

"It's different now," he interrupted. "You still don't grasp the situation. I worked the law on them before to get you free. But now they *are* the law and they can change it to counter one. It's like dancing on quicksand."

I took a chair, and again I was afraid, just a little, down deep where it hardly showed. This was beginning to feel like the inner world of Child's mind, where everything was solid and tangible, but where nothing could be trusted, where solidity could disappear, where liquid could become solid ground beneath the feet.

"She's not the only one," he said, as if mass suffering made her individual plight less important. It only made it more important.

"Let me have the phone," I said, reaching for it.

"Who?"

"Morsfagen."

"This might be a mistake."

"If the sonofabitch wants my esp, wants my work, then he is just going to have to see that she gets out of the Tombs!"

I found the number in Harry's private directory of unlisted phones, dialed it, and waited while a soldier called a noncom to the phone—while the noncom went and got a major who stuttered—and while the major finally went and summoned Morsfagen.

"What is it?" he asked. Cold. Deadly. Forceful. The sound of the well-trained bill collector.

"There's a girl being kept in the Tombs, charged with sedition, for god knows what reason. She——"

"Melinda Thauser," he said, cutting me short. He seemed to enjoy that. Like putting thumbscrews on me.

"I see you're up on things all around. Well, catch this, then. I want her released, and I want all charges dropped against her."

"That's beyond my control," he said—he did.

"It better not be."

"It is."

"It better not be, because you've just lost yourself an esper if it is."

"Services that can be commandeered in time of war— like an esper's services—are never lost," he said. Color him infuriatingly calm, cool, and collected. I wanted to kick his damned teeth in. He probably would still have smiled at me with *that* smile.

"Services cannot be commandeered unless the craftsman can be found," I said.

"Is this a threat to withhold services from the government in a time of national crisis?" he asked, smiling through every word. Snapping turtle mouth there, looking for one of my incautious fingers.

"Look," I said, trying another tack, "suppose we let the charges ride for the time being. Suppose the only thing that you concede is the bail. A low bail, but she'll still stand trial."

"Out of my control," he said again. But the tone of his voice said that nothing was ever out of his control.

"Like hell!"

"I'm not on the junta, you know."

"Look, Morsfagen, suppose she also destroys the damn book. Now it's the book she's in trouble for, isn't it? The first part of it?"

"With or without the book," he said, "the trouble remains for us. The danger does not lie within the printed page, but within the mind of the man setting words to paper. Or woman, as the case may be. But there isn't any use discussing it. I haven't any say about it. Besides, I've seen her picture, and I'm certain you can wait seven months for that kind of stuff." Voice of the obscene telephone caller, yet still authoritarian. In the back of his throat: unvoiced laughter that will explode when I hang up.

"I know why you're in the military now," I said, my voice deceptively neutral.

"Why is that?" he asked, walking into it.

"When your own manhood is negligible, a gun must at least be a little consolation." And I hung up on the creep.

"That was definitely a mistake," my mentor said.

I picked my coat up and worked into it. "Maybe."

"No maybe about it. Where are you going now?"

"Home, pack some things, and get out. Look, I'll get a message to you so you'll know where I'm at. Wait. Scratch that. I've got a key to Melinda's apartment. If it's still unoccupied, I'll stay there. They'll check hotels right away, so maybe her place is safer. Maybe I'm not as potent a wedge as I think I am. Maybe they really don't need my esp. But I rather think they'll come crawling after a while; it's the only way I can help her."

"You love her?" he asked.

I nodded. I couldn't really say it. Maybe it was still a hangover from my delusions of godhood. Or maybe I was just afraid that her affection did not run as deep as mine. Perhaps, in a month, she had forgotten me.

"Then hurry," he said. "You might not have much time."

I left his Tudor home under the trees, took one of his two hovercars, and pressed the accelerator half through the floor on the way home. The craft veered from one side of the road to the other as clouds of snow kicked up and stuttered through the blades of the air cushion mechanism, but I didn't hit anyone.

Perhaps the sole reason for Melinda's arrest was her own actions. But I thought not. It seemed too clever a hook in my side to hold me should I ever return from the noman's-land inside of Child. Melinda was the perfect insurance policy, they must have thought, against my temper and foolishness.

I parked the car on my patio and entered the house through the double glass doors, packed two suitcases, and folded the healthy amount of cash in my library lockbox into five different wads in five different pockets. It was all in Western Alliance poscreds, so the rise or fall of any one government could not much affect its value. I took two game pistols out of the collection in the shooting range downstairs, grabbed a box of ammunition for each, and put everything in the car.

As I drove off the patio and down the lane alongside the cliff which overlooks my segment of the Atlantic Ocean, the police made their appearance. At the foot of the drive, eight hundred feet below, a howler pulled into sight, lumbering upward in all its armored glory.

IV

I stopped the hovercar and watched the approaching vehicles, three in all: the howler which I had first seen, a crimelab truck full of detection equipment (though what they hoped to find here, I could not guess), and a regular patrol car with two plainclothesmen inside. They were sending heavy guns for a single man, and they had not wasted any time about it. I looked across the road at the woods, the sloping hill leading to other houses in the development, and knew the hovercar would never hold up on that terrain. The beaters need an even surface to work on. In hilly country, the four heavy blades would chew through a rise in the land, twist, slice up through the floor of the cabin and make it nasty for me, to say the least. And if I went back, there was only my house to take refuge in, for that was at the top of the cliff, with no road down the other side. I had paid for isolation, and now it was working against me.

The howler siren came on, as if I had not seen the damn thing and didn't understand its purpose. It was no more than three hundred feet away now, its great blades setting up secondary air currents which were beginning to rock my own hovercar.

Morsfagen was taking no chances. If I was under house arrest, locked up in the AC complex, there was no doubt that I would work for them, and there was no chance that I could stir up any sort of hornet's nest about Melinda Thauser. Perhaps it was the general himself in the last vehicle, come to smile that smile of his while they loaded me into the howler and took me quietly away.

But, bullheaded as I am, I was not about to make it that easy for them.

Call me heroic. Call me daring. Call me adventurous and devil-may-care. Actually, what I called myself at the time, under my breath, was "fool" and "congenital idiot" and "raving madman," but that is neither here nor there.

Turning the hovercar sideways to the lumbering howler, I backed across the narrow lane, aimed the nose of my craft at the brink of the cliff. For a moment, I almost lost my nerve, but my insanity (or heroism, if you will) took hold again, and I tramped the accelerator to the floor.

The drifting craft whined pitifully, shuddered as the blades roared with the flush of power. Then the hesitation was replaced by a burst of power, and the little car shot forward at top rev, cleared the edge of the cliff, and hung three hundred feet over the beach, a piece of delicate dandelion fluff—which turned abruptly into a lump of lead and dropped down, down, down like a goddamned stone.

I kept the accelerator to the floor, building a solid air cushion beneath. But I held the horizontal controls back against full stop so that none of the power could be used to drive the craft forward or backward—it all went straight down. The car pitched and yawed, but I pumped the correction pedal furiously, compensating for that.

The white sand rose, as if the beach moved while I hung in the same spot. If I had tried this maneuver a hundred feet closer to the house, there would not have been beach below, but great, shattered boulders. And the story would have ended much differently indeed.

The last thirty feet, the building column of air under

the car began to slow me. I braced myself for the jolt of contact, and hoped the blades would not be damaged too much. Then the rubber rim of the oval vehicle slewed into the sand, the blades whirled frantically and bit through the grainy earth. Showers of sand exploded into the air, blinded me on all sides with a white, rattling curtain. Then the blades kicked the craft off the earth and held it ten feet above, whirling madly. There was a ratcheting noise somewhere below, but it could not be that serious if the car still flitted and if I were still alive. I cut back on acceleration, and settled down to two feet above the flat beach.

Taking the car out next to the curling waves that foamed along the snow-layered shore, I looked up at the cliff to see what was transpiring there—and was just in time to watch the howler leap into the air in a blind rush to follow me.

Take a howler: five tons of armored vehicle; made to ram through walls if necessary, with huge blades that rev four times faster than a small car's blades ever can; extra compressed air jets placed around the rubber landing rim to add extra boost if the time should come when they are needed. Like now. And howlers make leaps off ten-foot embankments all the time when in pursuit of a man on foot or on a wheeled vehicle like a motorcycle. But ten-foot embankments in no way resemble three-hundred-foot cliffs. If my car had dropped like a stone, the huge howler fell like a mountain.

In three hundred feet, it was building so much speed and force that the blades at full and the compressed air jetting wildly would do nothing to stop its descent. I could see the drivers coming to the same conclusion. Behind the armored glass windscreen, they were screaming.

The fall seemed to take forever, though it could only have been seconds. The boom of the mammoth blades smashed along the cliff and cracked out across the sea like cannon volley. The compressed air jets whooshed with a decibel range that threatened to crack even the safety glass in the windows of my hovercar. I didn't want to see what was going to happen, but I could not take my eyes off that fascinating descent no matter how much I wanted to.

Down...
And down...

Sand exploded upward as the howler reached the beach.

But the thing wasn't slowed.

It struck the earth with a terrifying explosion of sound, with a screech of metal shredding, twisting, buckling in upon itself. The cab snapped off the cargo hold, leaped toward the water, plowed into the sand at more than forty miles an hour, carrying the dead drivers. It bulled its way thirty feet into the sea before coming awash in the water.

At the point of impact, the gas tank under the cargo section had split and the leaking fluid had touched some hot parts. There was a whoosh of red and yellow, and flames spiraled a hundred feet in that first moment of ignition. On the sand, coppers and parts of coppers who had been riding in the rear of the howler lay everywhere, burning as the fuel washed them and ignited on them. They were all dead already anyway, from the terrific impact of the crash.

Overhead, the crimelab truck and the hovercar perched by the edge of the cliff, their occupants looking down and gesticulating. None of them seemed interested in coming down, though the car with the plainclothes agents would have had every bit as good a chance of making it as I had had, even if that chance was not really so good at all.

The howler's descent, however, had been a good object lesson and the point had sunk in instantaneously.

I turned the car along the beach in the direction of the city, where I knew I could regain the highway before long.

In a very few minutes, they would have an alert out for me. I drove fast and tried to forget that war makes killers of all men, whether directly or indirectly. For isn't it true that every citizen who roots for "our side" to "kill the gooks" is as responsible for every death as the man wielding the gun? Isn't it true that none of us can escape responsibility for the madness of our species? Even those of us who live in carefully constructed shells, even we constantly affect the lives of others for evil. Existentialism? Maybe. But there on the afternoon beach, it helped me to recover my wits as I sped away from the flaming corpses behind.

As I drove, I grew more and more infuriated with myself, for I had been so smug about dealing with them—and yet I had not put any of that sense of assurance to work for me. It was time to stop feeling sorry for myself, time to make my anger into something more formidable than emotion.

I was superman, and it was time to act like one.

Or so I thought and so it seemed to be. . . .

V

In the large apartment complexes such as the one in which Melinda maintained her home, there is every convenience of modern living that one could wish for—all under a single roof. There are supermarkets and there are special "ethnic" food centers; there are clothing stores and beauty salons, bookstores and theaters, garages for hovercars and banks for money, bars for drinking and restaurants for nights out of the kitchen, office supply stores and car shops, electricians and plumbers and carpenters, legal prostitutes and drugbars for the purchase of approved chemical stimulants.

To connect all these facilities and to make them all accessible in minutes from every reach of the three-block-square structure (and when you consider that with eighty floors and nine square blocks per floor, there are 720 square blocks, you can easily envision how distant some points of the complex can be from others), there is a maze of express elevators, slow elevators, descending and ascending escalators, horizontal pedways with belts moving at a variety of speeds, and stairs—though very few of the last. Near any of the main shopping plazas within the structure, one needs only to stand close to any wall to hear the thrumming arteries of transportation moving ceaselessly, efficiently, like blood behind the plastic and the plaster.

It is possible to live in one such complex without ever finding the need to leave for wider spaces. If the urge to divorce oneself from civilization and its mad pace becomes too urgent, there are the underground parks with false sunlight and real trees and four floors of convoluted paths and bubbling, fresh brooks. There are butterflies and small animals and birds. If one happens to be a sports aficionado, there are arenas where various games are played out weekly. Some housewives who seek no career beyond that of running their home may be married in the complex church, return from a honeymoon, and perhaps live the next ten years in eighty floors, each nine square blocks. Husbands who work at stores within the complex and not at professions that take them into other parts of the city, may spend an equal length of time without ever seeing the real sky and the real world except through their windows—which usually exhibit other apartment complexes built nearby.

And no one seems to mind.

In fact, this sort of existence is advertised as a blessing, as something all of us should desire.

For instance:

Crime, the realtors point out, is all but nonexistent within the confines of the apartment area. All corridors are monitored by a full-time staff of police from central scanning depots within the structure. Anyone bent on illegal activity against the residents would find that it is utterly impossible to get into the complex without a plastic identicard full of computer nodes which activate the automatically locked doors. And only residents are carefully screened guests may have the use of such cards. Since everyone with a card has his fingerprints, retinal pattern, blood type, odor index, hair type, and encephalographic readouts on file with the structure's police bureau, it is difficult, if not impossible, to commit a crime from within and escape detection and retribution. Compared to the outside world, with its juvenile gangs, organized rackets, and political dissidents, such a style of crime-free living is quietly attractive.

Pollution, the same realtors say, is a serious problem outside the complexes. Man never really seriously stopped fouling his air and his water until the early 1980s. Then, some of the European and Asian countries had still not seen the light. Pollution had not totally ceased until the mid 1990s, after the complexes were being built. Outside, the air had still not been purified. The death rate for lung cancer, beyond the complex walls, among those unfortunate enough not to have seen the wisdom of such compact mini-cities, was three times that for complex dwellers. The same for all respiratory diseases. The realtors could go on and on. And they often did. The complexes had elaborate filtration systems, and this selling point was never overlooked.

Inflation, the salesmen will tell you, is far less noticeable in a complex apartment, for the companies who own the mammoth structures also do the buying from the smaller stores within. A company owning a hundred complexes, buying for a thousand grocery stores and hundreds of thousands of citizens can obtain lower wholesale rates and pass the savings on to the residents.

A community sense of togetherness, the realtors insist, has all but died in the regular life style, in the cities and the suburbs. There, they say with great sincerity, there is a dog-eat-dog, every-man-for-himself attitude. In the great complexes, this is not so. There is a camaraderie, a sense of group achievement, a community pride and identity that makes life more like it used to be: "Back When." No man need be an island, but a part of a great continent.

Trumpets. Drums. End of the ad.

Why don't I live in one, then? Why build a house by the sea, set in its own isolation of pine trees? Well, there are lots of reasons.

For instance:

Crime, it seems to me, is nothing more than a necessary evil, an offshoot of freedom and liberty. When you give a man a list of rights, things that he should expect to be able to do according to his standing as a member in the human community, you are providing the unscrupulous man with a list to stretch to his own ends. You are giving the clever man something to look over in search of loopholes. And, in the end, you have criminals making the free-enterprise system work for them, their way, as they understand it. So you arrest them and you punish them, but you learn to live with them. Unless you would prefer restricting those liberties everyone enjoys. You could shorten the list of rights or do away with it altogether, thus giving the unscrupulous ones less to stretch, less things to find loopholes in. Everyone suffers, of course, when the list is destroyed. And the cleverest and most intelligent of the unscrupulous manage to end up at the top of the pile anyway—or maybe they were the ones who eliminated the list of rights to begin with, in order to cut down on competition from amateurish punks. They call themselves "city government" and steal legally. And with their surveillance of the corridors, their bugging of elevators and escalators and pedways and stairs, their files on every resident, which grow thicker with data each year, the apartment complexes do not foster liberty, but slowly absorb it from their residents.

Pollution? Well, maybe I'll die of lung cancer sooner than a complex dweller. But I can breathe the smell of the sea, the smell of wet earth after a rain, the ozone produced by lightning. My air has not been so filtered and cleaned as to become flat and unexciting.

Inflation? Perhaps things *are* cheaper in the complexes, and perhaps that's because the companies really want to give their residents a fair shake in every way possible. But there is something frightening, to me at least, about depending on one conglomerate entity for your food, your drink, your entertainment, your clothing, your necessities, and your luxuries. I stopped being dependent on Harry, my father image, by the time I was halfway through adolescence. I don't yearn to be fathered or mothered to death by some team of accountants and cost-projecting computers.

A community sense of togetherness, they say, makes life much more fun in the giant apartment structures. But I don't want to have to be friends with *anyone* merely because I happen to live near them. I don't enjoy the high school rah-rah, go-team unison of small minds or the brittle-fingered canasta desperation of old people seeking companionship in their last days. Besides, last night, I saw an example of that community togetherness which banded the "innocent" citizens of that complex across the street into a spying, ruthless creature which could report neighbors to the police to have them slaughtered. Community togetherness can lead to a consensus outlook that seeks and destroys any dissident element, no matter how small and really harmless.

Thanks but no thanks.

I'll take my sea.

And my pine trees.

And even my damned polluted air.

Her apartment was as it had been. It did not look as if it had even been searched—a strange fact if they truly had thought her involved with revolutionary elements. I got some food in a plaza supermarket and returned to her place, fixed myself a solid meal, and ate until my shriveled stomach was somewhat back to normal size.

After that, I turned on the television and was instantly glad I had taken so many precautions getting here. I had driven to the airport, abandoned my hovercar, and had brought my luggage back here on a bus. If I had not been so quick and careful, I might now be jailed, for I was a television star it seemed, my face a portrait on the wide-angle tube.

On the news, they showed coppers at my house, looking busy as they attended complex machinery. They found signs of traitorous activities—signs which they had planted since my escape. They had uncovered a "secret room" and such nefarious things as a photo-printer and stacks of anti-Alliance, anti-military booklets I was alleged to have written with—they pointed out—the aid of Melinda Thauser, who had already been taken into custody. There were even weapons caches and a small bomb assembly bench. I was wanted on a warrant for sedition. Very neat indeed.

But there was another warrant as well.

The second one was for murder.

They exhibited, in ludicrous detail, the demolished howler at the foot of the cliff, the charred corpses of the men who had been riding in the back of it. They had fished the detached cab from the sea, and the drivers were laid side by side, horribly mutilated by the broken windscreen and the crumpled roof of their vehicle. According to the news, I had run the howler off the narrow cliff road. I had charged it directly, and when it was obvious I was going to hit them, the drivers of the mammoth rig had swerved off the road to avoid killing me. Quite gallant of them.

I waited for the reporter to say how I had managed to make my escape with still another cop car ahead of me, but he talked around it without letting the home audience in on the way I had dived over the cliff myself.

KELLY KILLER, COPS SAY! That was the headline the papers would carry, surely. Those boys always went for alliteration.

I spent most of the evening working over a plan in my head. Just remaining on the loose did not seem enough, any longer, not while Melinda was in the women's quarters of the Tombs, down there in dark, cold stones without me.

Somewhere around nine in the evening, my thinking was interrupted by the whine of sirens and the sinister rattle of gunfire.

I stood, listening intently, wondering if they were now surrounding the building, now getting wise to my sudden disappearance. But they would hardly be firing out in the streets. And there would be no need for sirens. Indeed, sirens would warn me, and such a building as this provided a great many hiding places.

Turning to the broad picture window, I looked down into the street eight floors below. Three howlers curbed in front of the building across the street, and uniformed coppers poured out of them like insects from a broken hive. From the fourth floor of that building, a number of men opened fire with small arms, pitifully insufficient against such organized and deadly police.

What followed was a bloody, desperate battle which carried no reason nor purpose to it, so far as I could see. Obviously, the people on the fourth floor were considered enemies of the state, for there was also an army car down there, with what appeared to be high brass directing the operation. But why tear gas was not used, why bullets were chosen instead, I could not understand.

I watched, terrified and fascinated.

In the end, as those on the fourth floor surrendered, tossing guns and ammunition down to the street, the most chilling scene of all occurred. Searchlights now illuminated the rooms beyond the shattered fourth-floor windows, showed the men and women there, dejected and defeated. Almost simultaneously, the inside doors to the building's corridors burst open, and uniformed coppers stepped into the rooms. They carried what appeared to be machine pistols, and they used them expertly, slaughtering the thirty or so human beings who had already surrendered. A tall, willowy blonde twirled gracefully and fell across the windowsill. Her long fingers scrabbled at the wooden frame, while her mouth went slack and her face contorted hideously with the knowledge of impending death. Another eruption of gunfire behind her sent her lunging through the window, tearing her arms on projections of broken glass. She tumbled sixty feet to the street, turning lazily, her waist-long yellow hair sprayed around her like a halo ...

At last I turned away from the window.

What I had just seen was a sample of that "community

camaraderie" the real estate agents spoke of. The neighbors of those dead men and women had turned them in, surely, in righteous indignation that a cell of revolutionaries should exist in *their* building.

The consensus had killed them as surely as the bullets.

The consensus, I would have to soon learn, was a living, breathing creature that could attack in vicious rage.

And the molders of the consensus had Melinda in a cell where they could get to her at any moment. . . .

VI

At a quarter to three in the morning, after a short nap and a quick snack of cheese and crackers, I dressed and slipped both loaded pistols into the pockets of the heavy coat I was wearing. Through a series of pedways, escalators, and elevators, I reached the ground level of the west wall of the apartment complex and went outside. For a moment, I savored the cool air, then turned right and walked briskly toward the center of the city. I held my chin high and made my step firm but not rushed. I tried to look as little like a fugitive as possible. In ten minutes, I passed a dozen other pedestrians without getting a second glance from any of them, and I thought the ruse was working.

Twenty-five minutes from her apartment complex, the squat, round surface portion of the Tombs hove into sight. This was the administrative wing, containing offices and files. Light burned in some of the long, narrow window slits. Below this modest and attractive nubbins, bored for dozens of levels into the earth, were the cells and the interrogation chambers. The place had been designed, originally, as a modern progressive prison. But slowly, through the years since the cold war had been renewed, it was converted into something quite less than progressive by those reactionaries who branded change as part of any enemy plot, labeled disagreement as subversion. The ideal of rehabilitation was abandoned by those who thought punishment was better than converting to usefulness. Frustration and boredom and rage were the companions of those locked within these walls.

And Melinda was there now.

There were three howlers parked along the curb, all of them empty and locked. At the four corners of the intersection, there were piles of snow which had not yet been removed. Streetlights threw long shadows against the circular structure. There was no other person in sight, and the scene was almost like still-life painting into which I had walked through some unknown magic.

I had both guns shoved into my overcoat pockets, though I prayed to an insane and unheeding God that I would not have to use them. Indeed, I didn't think I could use them if the occasion arose. But, clutched in my hands, they gave me a sense of determination, as the dying Catholic must feel when his fingers grip his crucifix and he doesn't feel so bad about meeting the end.

Stepping from the curb, I crossed the icy street toward the main entrance of the building.

The doors opened and two coppers came out, walked to the last of the three howlers, and got in.

I kept moving. Up on the other curb, across the sidewalk, up the long flight of gray steps, my heart pounding and my mouth dry. I pushed through the double doors into the well-lighted lobby of the place, took it all in as I walked across it, went down the main corridor to the elevator, which I took down to the cell levels. The doors opened on a guard sitting at a desk, and I received my first challenge.

"Yeah?" he asked, looking up from the magazine of undressed girls and overdressed fiction.

I probed out, struck into the center of his mind, fishing through the currents of thoughts there, seeking the fragments of scenery from his past and from the future he imagined for himself. I had not done this thing since I had been a child in the AC complex and they had made me do it in experiments. It was distasteful and painful, to me as well as to my victim. But I found the worst of his thoughts, the deepest id dreams which would horrify him and which would make him cringe with shame. The one I chose was of him and his eleven-year-old sister—a whip and a chain and all the horrors of sexual perversion those symbols represented. And I pushed them up into his conscious mind with such force that they became reality for him, so that he lost sight of me for only a split second and fell back, reeling, under the force of the ugliness which had welled up from the center of him.

Then I got out of there.

He was bent over the desk, clutching the corner of it, gagging, shaking his head, moaning to dispel the vision which he refused to believe could be his. I stepped forward, producing a pistol from my pocket, and struck him across the side of the head. He went down, hard, and stayed there. I wrestled him behind the desk, took off his jacket, ripped the arms loose, tied his ankles and wrists. I stuffed his handkerchief in his mouth, rolled the bulk of the jacket up, and tied the handkerchief in place.

And then I took his keys and opened the prisoner file, found her cell number. It was eight floors further down. Committed to this insanity now, I used another of his keys to open the restricted elevator which led to the lower levels. I went down.

When the elevator doors opened again, there was another guard waiting, though this one was more alert than the first. He looked at me and saw that I had not come with an escort, even though I was obviously not a regular traveler in these halls. He unsnapped his holster with a clean, swift move, slipped fingers over the butt of his gun with the reactions of a trained fighter.

I pried open his mind and found his id.

I wallowed in it.

I dredged up a vision of his own basic blood lust, a gruesome, mad match that even he would never have known existed inside him. It involved his unvoiced, unrealized, unknown desire to—as an adolescent boy—rise up in the middle of the night and slaughter both his parents in their bed. There were spraying blood, harsh and strangled screams, terrified faces of two gentle people, the boy's hands wielding an ax whose blade gleamed wickedly in the thin light which streamed through the bedroom window from the iron street lamp beyond. . . .

When I got out of his head, he had dropped his pistol and had turned to the wall, where, screaming, spitting, on the verge of losing his sanity, he smashed his fists into unyielding, gray concrete. I clubbed him mercifully with one of my pistols. The vision would not return when he woke, and he would probably not even remember what had given him his fit. But knowing that didn't make me feel any more heroic.

When he was tied and gagged, I took the cell block keys from the desk and wetn after Melinda.

She was sitting in her cell; her reading lamp was on, and she was absorbed in some propaganda literature she was permitted to read. I rattled the key in the lock and swung the door open before she looked up. When she saw it was me, she let her mouth hang loose some while before closing it and taking a much needed breath.

"If I'm interrupting a good book, I'll come back later," I said, nodding at the propaganda.

She threw it down. "That drivel is really fascinating," she said. "The guy who writes it is either the biggest con man in existence or he believes it himself—in which case he has to be a mongoloid idiot, no question."

"Aren't you glad to see me?" I asked. "Aren't you going to hug and kiss the hero in your midst?"

"You can't be in my midst, because I'm only one person, not a multitude. Though this goddamned prison baggies do make me look like more than one woman." She pulled at the uniform, shrugged. "You're here. I never expected you, don't know how you managed it, and doubt if we'll get back out. Like I said, the prison baggies here...."

I pulled jeans, sweater, and thin windbreaker from under my overcoat, all of which I had secreted there before leaving her apartment. "Do me the honor of a striptease?" I asked.

She grinned, stripped without asking me to turn my back (which I would have refused to do anyway), and dressed in the clothes I had brought.

I felt every inch the hero, all the while my mind was yelling "Fool" at top volume.

As she pushed past me to leave the cell, she stood on her toes a moment and kissed me, then turned quickly away again. Before she could take two steps, I grabbed her and turned her around. What I thought I had seen was in her eyes: tears.

"Hey," I said, feeling the male stupidity that cannot cope with tears. "Hey." Really stupid.

"Let's go," she said.

"Something wrong?"

"I've been wondering if you were alive, wondering if even you were whether you would care enough to come for me."

"But of course—"

"Shush," she said, stopping the tears. "We haven't time for this, have we?"

We closed the cell door and locked it, went up and past the other cubbyholes. Each was separated from the other by cement walls, but the fronts were all bars through which we could see the occupants. None of them, however, seemed to care much about us.

We went up in the first elevator, passed the first and second unconscious guards. When the second elevator opened on the main ground floor corridor, we walked briskly into the lobby, pushed open the glass doors and breathed in the cold night air. No one in the lobby or at any of the work desks paid the least bit attention to us. I took Melinda's arm, and we walked down the steps—

—just in time to confront General Alexander Morsfagen and four young and dedicated men with guns in their hands!

"Good evening," he said, bowing to us.

The four men with guns did not bow.

"I do believe you're surprised, Mr. Kelly. I didn't expect to see your cool broken like that." But whether or not he expected it, he certainly did enjoy it. His face was split with a grin you seldom see outside of mental wards.

"Who is he?" Melinda asked.

"Morsfagen."

"The title too, please," he said. But he was not just being humorous. His voice was stiff and deadly beneath the surface delight.

"General Morsfagen," I told her.

"And you're under arrest, of course," he said.

The four guards advanced on us, efficient but somehow less wary than they had been at first. It would have been possible, perhaps, to use my two pistols on the lot of them. They did not seem to expect that I might be armed, and with both my hands in my pockets and wrapped around the sweat-slicked butts of the weapons, they might have bought it but good before they realized what was happening.

Might have.

But nothing is certain.

Besides, the back of my mind played with the memory of those flaming corpses on the beach, with the picture of the howler drivers screaming as they fell to sudden death. I didn't want more blood on my hands.

I contemplated using my esp on them. But the problem was that I could only invade one mind at a time. I knew I could not work fast enough to incapacitate all of them before one of those four boys panicked and put a few rounds of hard steel into Melinda and me.

What had happened to the god?

What was this? Mere men overpowering me and outthinking me, me a god?

"This way, please," Morsfagen said.

We followed him.

VII

Morsfagen had directed the placement of armed soldiers in the storm drains under and within four blocks of the Tombs. He had positioned a man behind every one of the slit windows of the administration building where I might possibly be able to force entrance. Even in the maze of aluminum air-conditioning ducts which wound through the great structure, a hundred men waited in silence with their narcotics pistols drawn and their nerves honed to crisp attention. With all of this waiting for me, I had walked up the front steps and through the lobby as brazen as a man could be. But even that had been planned for, and a watch had been kept from one of the apparently empty howlers parked before the Tombs entrance. They had watched me go in, had identified me, had let me get the girl, had let me bring her out, and then had nailed us. Perhaps Morsfagen let it go on that long so that he could level charges of jailbreak against both of us on top of what the government already had drummed up. But I half thought that he wanted to humiliate me as much as anything. And he had.

They put us in a howler, took us through snowy streets to the AC complex. They took Melinda away to a separate preventive detention apartment and placed me in another, where there were no sharp instuments or windows.

"General Morsfagen will see you tomorrow," the guard told me as he left.

"Can't wait," I said.

The door closed, the lock snapped, and quiet descended.

I flopped onto the bed and listened to the springs whine, and I thought about what a stupid, fumbling idiot I had been, even with Child's intellect integrated with my own. I had gone back to the house to pack, even when I should have realized that they would be coming for me. That had ended in the deaths of an entire howler crew, smashed and burning on my beach. Then I had gone to the prison after Melinda, with my brilliant plan of boldness, though I should have known that they would have been expecting the unexpected. Perhaps part of the plan was based on Child's cleverness—but another part was based on my own impetuousness, and Morsfagen knew my personality like the back of his hand—or better.

Look at yourself, Kelly, I yammered inside my head. The only esper in the world, amplified by a partial absorption of the psychic energies of the most complete genius—and still a failure. Still charging around with delusions that invariably trip you up.

Before my meeting with Child and my therapy in the mechanical psychiatrist, I had been going on the assumption that I was some holy character, some bright and shining product of godly grace, the Second Coming. Basically, I had been nothing more than a man, and I had only suffered by my refusal to understand that. I blundered into things acting like a god, and when I got hurt or frightened, I couldn't cope. I had never prepared myself against hurt and fear, for I could not see where either commodity would impinge upon a god.

Now, with Child, I had unconsciously begun to accept the god role again. Smug in the knowledge that I was esper with a genius inside me, I slipped back into the habit of looking on lesser mortals with contempt. And in my self-assurance, I had failed to use all my talents and intellect, had underestimated my enemy as the first Cro-Magnons underestimated the Neanderthals for a while.

For a while . . .

I stood up, suddenly less angry than I had been, and more determined. Okay, so I was not a god. I was not omniscient and omnipotent and superior to the military. I could not excuse past stupidity, but I could improve my outlook until I was able to be something which they could not cope with. The reason Morsfagen and other men could trip me up was simple to see: they were less powerful men, but they were fully developed, capable, and sure and confident. And I was fractured and unsteady and filled with doubts beneath the sheen of smugness. It was time to get to know myself, understand what I was and what I could expect to accomplish. After countless circuits of the main room of the apartment, I sat down on the bed again and relaxed. And that night, I came to know myself better than I ever had in my life.

I turned esp fingers back among the streaming thoughts of my own conscious mind. It was something I had never attempted before, though it now seemed the most natural exercise in the world. Perhaps I had always felt that I knew what I was thinking, that I was aware of myself. But, of course, like every man, I hadn't the faintest damn idea of what was going on inside my head. Head-tripping in countless other minds, I had left the territory of my own thoughts sacrosanct. Perhaps because I was afraid of what I might find.

In those rambles, stirring down into my own id and ego and superego, I found that I was purer, cleaner, less rotted than I might even have hoped for. There were things, of course, that terrified me and revolted me. But I took heart in that they indicated my basic humanness, my basic brotherhood with men, despite the fact I was made from chemical sperm and chemical ovum.

In that one long night, I finally understood the nature of society as I never had before. I had wrongly judged men. I had labeled them as inferior to me, when this was not the case. Some were inferior, some my equal, some even my superior in ways. Each minim of intelligent life on this planet was such an individual spark, such a varying quantity and quality that no sweeping comparison could ever be made. What I had always sensed and what I had misinterpreted was that *society* was inferior to me. No man. *Society*.

Society was an agglomeration of individuals equaling

less than its separate parts. In governments and institutions, the men chosen to rule, chosen to make policy and enforce decision, were those elected by the society that supported them—and because each member of society is different, because some median must be reached through the ballot, mediocre men assume office. The very intelligent vote for the intelligent candidates, but no one else does, for everyone else distrusts intellect. The reactionary and blind vote for their own slogan shouters, but no one else does. In the end, the people in the middle range elect their people, simply because they are in the majority. We get the mediocre. And because the mediocre are ill-gifted to deal with the problems of all factions of society, they make bad government and bad institutions. They distrust the intellectual and do not rely upon his wisdom. They fear the reactionary and the blind because such people threaten progress (a commodity the middle has been told to embrace all its life). They repress the intellectuals and the reactionaries and embrace their own people. But because they are mediocre, their own people are not served well, and corruption flourishes. Where each individual of society may be capable of governing his own sphere, the agglomerate government is incapable of governing anything except through intimidation and pure luck.

It may have been something that most people understand early in life, but it was a revelation to me. To win the games of existence, one must not attempt to fight by society's rules, because in most cases, one is fighting individuals, and not society. To win, one must attack the game on individual terms—not against a stereotype, not against a societal image, but against the other man, the single adversary.

The way to deal with Morsfagen was not as a tendril of the military plant, but as a man. His weaknesses did not lie in his adherence to the consensus—the consensus was too huge ever to be weak at all—but with himself, in his own human psyche.

Still, my problem was not solved. If I was not god, not the superior creature I had thought I was, how could I act at all? How could I function as an ordinary man? From birth, I had come to think of myself as something special, something sacred and superhuman. The attempt, now, to operate as just another man, would run against the grain of a lifetime of smug theory and self-delusion.

And then, quite suddenly, I knew what I had to do. It came like the nick of a razor in the morning, making me jerk with more surprise than it deserved. I should have understood what had to be done some time ago. I had to, finally, become the supreme being, the god, that I had always thought I was!

I began pacing the room again. My feet swished on the thick carpet. A clock ticked in the wall. Otherwise: heavy silence.

Be God . . .

God lay inside Child's mutant body, insane as He had always been, trapped as Child and I had been for that month. And though I did not want His madman's personality, I could make a great deal of use of His psychic energy. It was there to be tapped, the power that had made worlds, had generated galaxies and universes, that had established the infinitely fine balance of the cosmic scale. I could delve back into Child's twisted body and find the core of God's being, absorb Him and dissipate Him throughout my own mind, as I had Child. God would be part of me, a deeply threaded part without His own identity. I would, indeed, for all purposes, be God.

I could not sleep for the rest of that night. I wanted to see Morsfagen, wanted to try to work him as a human being long enough to have him get me to Child. Then, once he had done that, I would not have to deal with him on a man-to-man basis. I would be above that.

I was frightened that night, seeing hulking creatures in every shadow. In God's mind, down in that colossal id and ego, what would things be like? Would I be able to handle them, or would I be swamped and driven down, consumed? I forced the latter possibility from my mind and thought more positively. But the fear remained. It was not unlike the fear a child feels the first time he enters a great cathedral and sees the towering, somewhat menacing figures of the saints carved in great pillars of marble.

Morsfagen came at nine o'clock, smiling. "I thought you'd like to hear today's schedule," he said.

I said nothing, playing the role I had decided on.

"We start with a press release about the gun battle you had with the police last night. Did you know that you were seriously injured in that, perhaps fatally injured?"

He wanted some response that he could slap me down for, but I didn't give him the satisfaction. I accepted.

"Later in the day, we'll release some film of that shootout," he said. "We've already staged it. Looks very real with lots of blood. We found a fairly good double for your part, and we kept him mostly in the shadows so that it's hard to tell, really, who he is."

I said nothing.

He shuffled the papers in his hand, went on. "According to the reports, three officers will have died under your guns. We've made up life histories for them, all very touching. Two of them had large families and one had a brother who was a priest. We've put together composite photographs of various real officers to release to the press. Later tonight, word will be flashed to an outraged nation that you have died on the operating table. Even though you slaughtered the howler crew and three other policemen, we were trying to save you, see? Now, the first order of business today is for you to come along and help us film the operating room sequences. A double won't work in bright lights. I hope you can die convincingly, or at least pretend to look dead while you're lying there. Otherwise, you'll have to be drugged for it.

He stopped, watching me. It was time for my part, and my lines were crystal clear to me. "Look, how about a bargain," I said. I sounded fairly desperate.

He smiled. He was eating this up. Morsfagen's weakness was not in his rigid acceptance of military codes and consensus views, but in his need for power over other human beings, his delight at being on top of another man. I was giving him exactly what he wanted.

Maybe he would just hang himself with it.

"I fail to see," he said, "just what you have to bargain with." He motioned around at the windowless walls.

"Something you don't know," I said. "Something that, if you knew, would help you a great deal."

He frowned, smiled again. "And what would you want for this valuable piece of information?"

"My freedom. Melinda's freedom. We'd stay in the city. I'd do whatever you want."

"Oh, I hardly believe you would," he said.

"Look, Morsfagen, I'm not kidding you. I have something to tell you that could make a very big difference to the Alliance. I am not lying, and you must believe that."

"I'd love to hear it," he said, dragging this out to relish

every moment of my groveling. "But you must choose some other reward besides your freedom."

"Let the girl and me live here together. At least don't keep us in separate apartments."

He smiled, seemed to consider it. "All right. She is some nice piece, I'll tell you. That ought to be a big enough reward. Now tell me what this secret is?"

I started to speak, then stopped abruptly, just as I had planned, examining him with a great deal of suspicion. I must have looked pathetic, hunched there on the edge of the bed, unshaven, trying to bargain for petty favors that would come without question to a free man. It was the image I wanted him to have of me. "How do I know I can trust you?" I asked. "How do I know you'll keep your promise?"

He laughed sharply, deeply. "You don't."

"But that's not right!" I said. There was just the edge of a whine in my voice. I was a broken man, yes I was. I was just so many pieces for him to break further into dust.

"Fairness doesn't apply here," he said. "You'll just have to trust me. Or forget it all."

I hesitated. "I have nothing to lose, I guess," I said. "So I'll tell you." I hesitated again. Then I spoke: "I lied to you when I saw it was dangerous for me to go back into Child's mind. I just said that to get back into my own body and to get out of the AC complex. I can go back into him any time that I want, and I can bring a great deal of valuable data out to you."

He burst into loud, almost uncontrolled laughter, his face growing red. He slapped his sides with his hands, almost dropping the sheaf of papers, and finally the laughter turned into a choking cough. When he looked up at me again, he said, "I thought that much all along. I hadn't yet decided to risk sending you back, 'cause you're too valuable to lose. In a police state, an esper has more duties hunting the enemy at home than abroad. Now I can take the risk and clean out that freak's mind too. I thank you for your kind assistance in this decision." He nodded sarcastically.

"When will the girl be brought to me?" I asked, though I knew the answer already.

"You trusted me," he said. "I appreciate that. It shows that we will be getting along better than anticipated."

"I hope so."

"But there is one thing I think you should learn, for your own good," he said. He waited until there was no alternative but for me to ask him what that lesson was.

"What's that?" I asked.

"Trust no one," he said. "The girl will remain in a separate apartment."

I made a lunge for him, and the guard beside him slapped me across the face with the butt of a rifle. It was a deal more than I had bargained for. My jaws snapped together, banging my teeth painfully into my gums. I saw stars, multicolored one with a thousand points each, and crashed back onto the bed.

I tasted blood, spat it on the sheets. It was curiously bright there, glistening.

"Have you learned the lesson?" he asked.

"You lied," I said.

"I guess you've learned the lesson, then."

"That all military men are emasculated power freaks who can't make it with a woman but dig beating up on other men with guns."

"Keep it up," he warned.

"Sexless bastard!" I hissed.

"Larry," he called to the young soldier. The boy stepped forward, holding his rifle ready. Morsfagen motioned to me, quite the cavalier, and conveyed the necessity of what must be done.

Larry took two more paces, stepped in front of me, drew the rifle over his head—all of this happening so slowly, so measuredly that it seemed like a ballet—and brought the square butt down on my left shoulder so hard that I felt tissue separating.

I did not see the pretty stars at all this time, only a velvety and total darkness....

When I woke up, it was to the acrid odor of smelling salts which I rebelled against, gagging and pushing back from the stuff. But aside from that quite natural rejection, I offered no opposition. For the moment, Morsfagen was convinced he knew me. He suspected nothing and thought my anger was genuine.

I followed docilely to the corridor, the elevator, and the filming studios, where I played dead for them. Quite convincingly, he told me. They even let me bleed a little for them....

By late afternoon, the films had been made. There was a team waiting to rush the product to the city's main broadcasting facilities, where it would be shown for the edification and entertainment of the consensus citizenry sitting safe at home this night.

From there, we went to Child's room, where nothing had changed: lights dim, bedclothes rumpled, the mutant husk still lying there in the smell of sickness, antiseptics, and starch.

"Are you ready?" Morsfagen asked.

I'm not only ready, but anxious! I thought. But I did not say anything. It seemed the time to be petulant, snippy, moody. And he seemed to relish my performance.

The lights were dimmed, the recorders started, Child raised a little in his bed, and I was at last within reach of the godhood I had been seeking all my life. . . .

FOUR
Man As God...

I

I touched the sheen of His mental surface, drew back from the cold, humming tune of ultimate power.

In the darkness of the empty conscious mind, I hovered over the bending amber shell, slid along its eternal curve toward the horizon which always danced just beyond my grasp. In time, I found the weak spot on that amber smoothness, saw the moving shadows of things beneath, of things in the id and ego below. I pried at that weak spot, slit it open, sailed through and into God's mind....

Imagine:

Imagine the largest mirror in the universe, a million light-years from edge to beveled edge (no matter who the artisans were who created such a marvel, it is only the mirror itself which engages us). On such a great glass, there would be literally countless millions of visions, bits and pieces of colorful landscapes and peoples, events and futures and pasts and even moments of sundry present-times. Further imagine a cosmic hammer as large as a star (again, we care not of the men who forged that instrument, but only of its actions) brought to bear on the very center of that fantastic mirror. And then imagine the flying shards of silvered glass clattering down, down, down into the bottom of Existence, to the end of Time, and there to lie in pools of pitch blackness with their wild reflections frozen in them.

This was the mental landscape inside of Child this time, far different from what it had been. It was a mind of superhuman dimensions, fractured into near uselessness, the mind of God, the Being who had made the Earth, the galaxy, the universe, and each of us in it, the god who had forged the first DNA and RNA and begun the craziest dream ever. And yet it was the most disorganized place I had ever seen—disorganized and brilliant at the same moment, wilder, stranger, more fearful than any mind I had seen in all my years of head-tripping.

I settled through glazes of amber . . .

. . . through ice spicule clouds the color of freshly spilled blood . . .

. . . through a fine blue fog and finally down into the smashed visions of this mad universe . . .

For a while I hung there, feet of my analogue body inches above a glittering shard of stars. Then I touched bare toes on galaxies and walked across the ruined skies to another fragment, this a jungle scene with strange birds and stranger ambulatory plants. I seemed to settle down into the jungle, to become a part of it, though the moment I wished to go on I ceased this empathy and rose until I stood above it, looking down on it—and looking out on the millions of other scenes awaiting me on the flat black table of nothingness.

I set out, searching for the core of God, for the shattered glass that held Him.

He could not be far.

Wasn't God everywhere?

I walked through a place of flowers where the earth was as thick as water reeds with boles as large around as two men could link their arms. The leaves were high overhead and did not allow even a minim of sunshine through.

I walked through a place of flowers wher the earth was carpeted with an explosion of ripe colors, where clouds of spores rose and swept by me as their season came, where seeds stuck to my analogue body from the sappy tendrils of man-sized milkweed plants.

I saw a red sky with a blue sun, and the land was parched and empty beneath both.

Twice as I wandered, I felt His onrushing presence, the huge power of His disabled mind. I reached out, grasping blindly for Him, but He was gone in the instant, leaving me groping and frustrated.

Several times, the sky itself came screaming down, compressing the air beneath it until my analogue body threatened to explode. The sky shattered around me, was resurrected as flocks of blue-white birds, and rose again to hang high over everything.

The earth rose and fell like a beating breast, the vibrations of the heart muscle coursing through me.

There were creatures with many eyes, others with more legs than I could count.

Dead birds fell from the sky by the tens of thousands, became lizards when they struck the earth, climbed the rocks about me, grew wings, and entered the clouds again.

There were places where the trees wailed and broke open with ugly sores, bled as if they were made of flesh. The dripping blood became crimson pebbles where the tree touched the earth.

I stalked through this chaos, searching.

At last, I came upon Him where He was desperately trying to coalesce into an analogue form with which He could contact me. He was a smoky, bluish pillar of psychic energy, roiling, tumbling, spitting sparks of many colors, at last jelling into the shape of a man: Buddha.

"It is a wise man who knows how to compromise," Buddha said, rubbing His large bare belly and smiling down at me. He towered twenty feet into the air.

"I will not compromise," I said.

"The seven lives——"

I pushed on. "I will not compromise." I extended fingers of my own psychic energy, and felt out the core of God, seeking for the pattern to its structure.

The figure shifted, became an image of Jesus Christ. "Truly, I say unto you, a man who recognizes his own mortality is a happier man. A man who comes to live with his weakness with all humility is a man destined for my kingdom."

I grasped Jesus' neck with psychic hands and throttled Him.

He exploded, whirled into a column of energy, a furious, storming energy that longed to strike out at me but could not. Power is useless without a mechanism to harness and control it, and His mechanism had long ago deteriorated beyond the point of effectiveness. God was a hugely powerful pool of psychic energy without a manipulatory system: a car without wheels.

I reached with my own mental tendrils, and oblivious to the halfhearted and misdirected weapons He brought to bear against me, also oblivious of His pitiful pleading, I threaded him. He wanted to maintain His power, even though He was insane, and I could not make Him understand that it was time for a new God.

He wriggled and twisted in a vain attempt to pull free of me.

As I encircled Him, I knew that God had been insane long before Child had ever approached Him, had been a raving and incoherent mass of energy for—perhaps—millennia. All mankind's faiths had failed to understand the basic reason for chaos, for blind violence and hatred. We had attributed all the bad things of this world to "divine tests" of man's will and courage. But all of that was a theological falsehood, for the force energizing the universe was madness, not reason; insanity and not mercy. The madness had reached even the smallest particle of His being, aged like wine into the purest elements of horror.

Here died Jesus.

And Mohammed.

Here died Buddha and Yahweh.

But it was not all a loss.

For here, at last, I was born in my new image, to replace half a thousand false gods.

Burn the old altars and prepare new ones. Council your children with different commandments and slaughter the freshest of your lambs so that I may taste their blood in the morning dew.

I bled His energy away just as I might have tapped a dynamo or a battery, distributed it through my own psychic power until He was no longer a separate entity but merely another area of my own mind, as Child now was, another rising bank of power cells to draw upon for the creation of miracles. Not a shred of His personality or self-awareness remained; for all purposes, He had died—or had been transubstantiated, which was all the same now. His memories had been evaporated, and only the magnificent white brilliance of His power remained, condensed, purified, and made ready for use. For my use. It was now, after all, my power.

I had killed God, quite simply, just as I had killed Child some days before.

I felt no remorse.

Does one feel remorse when one shoots down a maniac

who is wielding a gun in a crowded department store?

Man as God. I retained the mortal form and the mortal outlook, with the enotions and the prejudices of men. I did not think that would be a weakness, but that it might actually make me a more benevolent and stable deity than the previous owner of my power had been. Man as God...

I vaporized the glittering metal analogues held in the fragments of mirror to my right. They disappeared without sound or light. I spread my hands, as in addressing the multitudes, and eliminated all the other pieces of that cosmic mirror.

There was total darkness drawing down about me like an oiled curtain.

I made light.

With the light, I fashioned stairs leading upward into further regions of darkness.

I walked out of there, erasing the stairs behind me.

Outside, the world awaited me, unknowing but soon to learn....

II

When I returned to my own body, carrying the power with me, the first thing I saw was Child's mutant shell convulsed with a series of hideous spasms that made it look much like the flickering, shape-changing image in a funhouse mirror. It sat straight up in bed, quivering like the shaft of an arrow. Its eyes were wide for the first time, the pulsing veins visible in the whites. Its slitted mouth worked furiously, though no words issued from it, no sounds at all. It scrabbled at its chest with two bony hands, clawed at its horrible face so viciously and persistently that blood seeped from the long red welts it carved in the flesh there.

The doctor attending the mutant grabbed it and attempted to force it backward onto the mattress, where restraining straps could be applied. But it heaved the white-smocked figure aside as if the man were so much paper, in an exhibition of strength that no one could have expected from such an emaciated body, from such skinny arms and powerless hands.

A dry rasping-hacking sound emanated from the creature's throat, but no words formed. It could have been tissue ripping under some unimaginable inward pressure rather than a conscious exercise of vocal cords.

"What's going on here?" Morsfagen demanded, rising from his chair with that slow, powerful, and somehow contemptible grace of his, cutting air like a sail.

The soldier named Larry came across the room, looking confused but determined. He dropped his rifle, and reached for the mutant. The creature snapped at him, sunk teeth into his wrist, and made blood fountain up brightly. The soldier screamed, struck at the mutant's face, smashed the jawbone. The mouth relaxed, released him, but the mutant was still awake, still struggled to gain control of itself and of the situation it found itself in.

"You did this!" Morsfagen roared, turning on me, pointing with a hand that trembled uncontrollably.

"No," I said quietly.

"You'll pay! Damn you, you'll see the woman raped for this, you'll see her humiliated!"

I could not even summon up the slightest bit of disgust for him. I looked with the eyes of the man I had been, but with the judgment of a god, and I could do no more than pity him. In a way, I resented my benevolence. I had longed for the power to strike back with thunder and with lightning. But now that the time had come, I found him deserving of scorn and pity more than wrathful vengeance.

"What is wrong with him?" he asked, shoving his broad face square into mine.

I knew exactly what was happening with Child's husk, though the rest of them could never possibly strike upon the truth. When I had left that shell, I had momentarily forgotten something which I should have remembered. There was still one portion of Child's mind down there in the black waste of his body: the id. All those scorpion analogues which I had dispersed in the ice-floored subterranean cavern so long ago were now risen up and in command of the mutant flesh. Normally the most directly impotent of the mind's factions, it now reigned without control, without opposition. But the id alone was not a functioning consciousness and could never hope to control the body: the Dr. Jekyll and Mr. Hyde syndrome was a complete impossibility, something that could only exist in fiction. The mutant husk would die now, days after its mental expiration, with the scorpion-clawed id seeking control to gratify its sex lusts and its blood longings.

"Everyone grab him at once!" Morsfagen directed, leading the others in on the bed.

The mutant thrashed wildly, pitched from side to side of the bed. Finally, it grasped the rails and clambered against them, flung itself over the side. It crashed onto the floor with a sickening crunch of flimsy bones, biting at the air, spitting blood across the tiles, clawing and weakly kicking at anyone who tried to bend to it, or to give it assistance in its time of need. To the id, there was no such thing as a friend, and it acted accordingly.

Then it succumbed.

Quietly, like a sigh.

Motionless on the hospital floor, with smears of blood marking the space around it, it seemed more like a squashed insect than the ex-home of a human creature.

They stared at the corpse for a long while, transfixed, perhaps, by its inhumanness. Then Morsfagen turned to look at me with the malevolence I had once despised.

"You killed him," he said matter-of-factly, beyond hatred now. He turned to the soldier named Larry. "Arrest him. Get that bastard out of my sight!"

Larry lifted his gun, grinning. He enjoyed using it too much. As he advanced on me like a homicidal maniac, I began to think that even the mindless shell of the mutant had been more human that this boy. Behind those eyes, there was something a little less than a man.

"Stop where you are," I said.

But he did not, of course.

I reached out for him, touched him, took him. His face went utterly blank, and he ceased his advance.

"What the hell—" Morsfagen began.

With other esp fingers, I touched the minds of everyone in that room and delivered them into a state of sleep which was not quite sleep, closer to death but not quite death. There, they would be far out of my way so that I might concentrate on the work ahead. Cautiously, I entered their minds with an ability I had never had before: neither in scope nor in power. I spread out their lives, their neuroses and psychoses, and I carefully untangled the knots that had warped each man and woman's psyche over the years. When they woke, they would be emotionally and mentally stable for the first time. The old fears and worries would no longer plague them, and their personalities (which had been structured all their lives to nurture the needs which were produced by those fears and worries) would be drastically reshaped. But for the better, surely—for the better. I was God, and I could not make mistakes.

Otherwise, why would you worship me?

I departed from the minds in the room, though I did not summon anyone back to consciousness. I did not need their help to command the tides and to grow storms in the heavens—nor for the much broader changes I wished to bring about in the world.

I settled down to bringing a new face to the Earth, enjoying every moment of my godhood—perhaps too well. . . .

III

And there, in that hospital room in the upper floors of the Artificial Creation complex, with the dead and bleeding mutant form before me, I knew the greatest triumphs of my entire life. I ranged far from those white walls, though I never once rose from the chair in which I sat. I flew over seas and continents without benefit of a body—without even an analogue form—to contain my psychic energies. Miracles were within my grasp now, and though I did not change any water into wine or raise any men from the dead, I did other things, yes, other things. . . .

The first order of business, so far as I was concerned, was to reach downward through the floors of the great structure and locate that place where I had been born, where plastic womb had contained me and where wired uterus had spit me out. It was no sentimental journey, no longing for a return to those cold mother walls, but the bitter-sweet taste of a deeply abiding vengeance.

I sent my awareness drifting down through the layers of the huge building, through plaster and lath, plastic and steel, through electrical conduits and wads of fluffy insulating material. I passed the radiating awareness of other human beings, but did not stop to handle them just yet, bent on the confrontation I had dreamed of for years.

Oedipal?

Not exactly. I did not want to kill my father and marry my mother, merely to kill my mother and be free. Certainly, there was a quality of love in it too, but that was easily overlooked.

I found the lowest two floors, where the paraphernalia of the genetic engineers cored the walls like fungus, filaments threaded through the plaster like disease worms. Machines descended from the ceilings of the rooms, thrust upward from the floors. There were blocks of data processing computers, memory banks and calculating components which handled everything from temperature regulation to DNA-RNA balance in the chemical sperm and egg. Along the walls and on various raised platforms around the floor there were programming keyboards for the men and women who maintained the delicacy of the computers' decisions.

In every great chamber, the center of attention was the womb itself. It was contained in a large, square glass tank whose exterior walls were more than three inches thick. Between these outer petitions and the meat of the nut, there were thinner layers of grass along with fiberglass wads of insulation. In the center were the nonconductive plastic walls, cored with the miles of wires reporting conditions back to the computers. There were electrode nubbins there by the tens of thousands, and waldoes so minuscule as to be unbelievable were doing impossibly tiny things to impossibly tiny creations, spheres of cells not yet remotely shaped like human beings.

Mother . . .

The womb, darkness, quietude, thrumming pulse of hidden works felt more than heard . . .

There were more than eighty technicians and medical

attendants clustered in the rooms of the genetic engineering equipment, all of them busy. I reached out with my godly esp and took control of every one of their minds. Work ceased; conversation broke off in midsentence. I directed them out of that place, upward through the building to regions of safety.

I surveyed the place as a sense of power stirred in me the like of which I had never experienced before. It was not the magnitude of the feeling, but the quality which made it so different. For the first time, I understood my godhood in a personal sense, understood that revenge was possible on a scale that I had never before comprehended. I had not been able to release that pent-up vengeance on a man, like Morsfagen, because pity had outweighed anger. But I could never pity a machine, a thing without feelings. I realized that my vengeance would always have to be directed against ideas and things and constructions borne of those ideas rather than against men; all men were pitiable in their stupid blindness to fact, but the creations of that stupidity, the ideas and ideals based on that stupidity deserved nothing but loathing and condemnation.

For a moment, I had the fleeting thought that this sense of power over the artificial wombs was much like the sense of power which the young guard at the Tombs had experienced in his fantasies about slaughtering his parents in their bed. Like him, I was rising up against the most fundamental loyalty of my life, against the salty seed and the warm womb which had engendered me (albeit, with the aid of some eighty technicians and physicians and computer programmers). But I thrust that notion down and got on with the job at hand.

I raised my figurative ax over my mother's symbolic head and savored the destruction I was about to wreak....

Did Jesus think of striking Mary down? Hardly. But I had given up that vision of God. I was another sort altogether.

I split open the surfaces of the walls and peeled back the plastic and the plaster, revealed the snaking conduits and the tangled ganglion of wires. I grasped these nerves gleefully and tore them free of the womb structures, sent the complex mechanisms into shuddering, heavy spasms of mechanical terror and confusion, into wrenching machine agony that drew smoke rather than blood or tears.

Moving swiftly, almost manically, I wrenched the programming keyboards loose of their connections and smashed them repeatedly into the floor.

The wombs were no longer connected to a brain to tell them what to do with themselves.

Smoke rose from the blocks of data-processing equipment, and tapes whined senselessly through the memory banks, seeking answers that could not be found.

There was but one answer, and that answer was God, and that God was me. . . .

I shattered the glass outer walls of all the wombs.

The floor was littered with fragments of sharp, bright, and bloodless flesh.

I broke inward, reached the heart of each warm, dark chamber, and shredded the slowly forming germ cells, squashed them.

I destroyed the wombs from inside, working back toward the shattered outer walls until there was nothing left but powder and fumes.

It must have looked singularly strange in that place: invisible hands making havoc in the center of that technological wonder; explosions without origin; plastic dribbling down and lying in cooling puddles on the floor; smoke rising everywhere. . . . It must have looked as if Nature had risen up in fury to dispose of such a blasphemous and pretentious project as this last folly of man's.

In essence, that was exactly what had happened.

Mother was dead.

And she was disfigured.

I had never had a father.

I left that place of smoldering memories, of twisted plastic and running wires, jellied tubes and transistors, returned to the hospital room where my body sat in the same chair where I had left it. Morsfagen and the others remained in a state of suspended animation, offering no resistance.

In a few moments, I had made all the necessary decisions; I knew what had to be done next. I had decided everything with the speed and the thoroughness of a super-computer, my thought processes racing faster and faster as the godly power within me became further integrated with my own mind. And I knew there were no flaws in my plans.

A god is not plagued with doubt.

I divorced my mind from my body again, and sought out of the AC complex, across vast stretches of land toward the minds of other men, where I would begin to build the new world. I found the members of the junta, one by one, and altered their minds. I rooted deeply, found their personality problems and removed them. I gave them the best psychotherapy man had ever imagined, and left them without a desire to rule.

Then, in each man's mind, I planted the desire for a return to elective government, and left them as their own counter-revolutionaries.

Next, I began a methodical search of the corners of the world; I radiated a growing, toughening web of power that sought out the minds of every leader in every nation, down through the lowest bureaucratic posts. I cleared those minds of power-hunger, of sexual frustration turned into violence. I healed them like a prophet with the power of god in his hands, and I left them better men.

Not satisfied yet, I struck downward and located all the men with the potential of leadership, even though they were not yet in positions to guide the destinies of their fellow citizens. I cleaned house in every psyche, helped all of them to learn to cope with existence and with their own place in the scheme of things.

And still my power grew. Or, perhaps, the more I used it, the better my manipulatory mechanisms became.

Next, I found the stockpiles of nuclear weapons hidden in all corners of the globe. I turned the fissionable material into lead by making Time flow a million times faster around the vicinity of the weapons. In the biochemical warfare laboratories, I destroyed all the mutant strains of death that scientists had generated. I opened the minds of those same scientists and cleansed them, made them reject the need to create death in order to feel worthy and powerful.

And the day wore on.

And evening came.

Still, I toiled.

It was somewhere beyond midnight when I finished reshaping the world and returned to my body in the AC complex. With all that I had done, I still felt energetic. None of my vitality had been sapped; it even seemed to have been magnified. The power I wielded was now more complex and enormous than I could ever have imagined.

I stretched my esp out and lingered along the surface of the moon, looking firsthand at the craters with eyes I constructed from the cold vacuum of space.

Stars winked close at hand, warm and yet freezing, pricks of light, yet mammoth stars.

I sped outward to them.

I touched red giants and white dwarfs, plummeted through the center of a sun, listening to the songs of exploding hydrogen, to the creation of matter, and to its instant destruction—or, rather, to its instant conversion into light and heat.

Energy...

I seemed to gain energy from every source I approached. My own light was brighter than that from any star, and was controlled far more intricately, making it more deadly and more important than countless suns in mindless eruption.

I passed outward beyond the galaxy.

I reached the end of the universe, sped through impenetrable walls of pearl gray, kept on going through dimensions until I reached another plane of creation.

And then I came back, skipping from galaxy to galaxy— then from star to star—then from planet to planet, finally back into the room where my mortal shell sat stupidly.

I rose up from the chair and left that room after turning Morsfagen and the others loose. I walked down the corridor and found Melinda's rooms, opened the door without touching it, and walked inside. I could have come to her with my mind, but I wanted the personal touch of flesh on flesh for this last and intimate step of the plan.

"You're free," I said as she turned from her window and looked at me, grinning her beautiful grin.

She started toward me....

And then I was to learn just how lonesome and awful the role of a god can be. I was about to meet with my first near-disaster since I had claimed the power....

IV

We were strangers.

We had made love and been in love, had shared secrets and dreams. I had risked my life for her, and she had done the same for me, though in a different manner. And yet, I did not know her. She seemed like a crippled doll, speaking with the voice of some hidden puppet-master who was a terrible craftsman and who was even worse at writing dialogue for his wooden creatures to perform on stage.

Everything she said seemed witless and stupid and—perhaps most unforgivably of all—utterly boring. I could not understand how such a woman could ever have interested me, even for the brief moments of lovemaking. Surely I had never been so anxious for the feel and taste of flesh that I had wooed and taken this creature in my arms! That seemed, now, like nothing more than animal-loving—bestiality.

In my arms, she was a pet.

And nothing more.

Yet I knew what she had once been, and I understood that she could again be important to me. I was certain, all at once, that all that was required was a change of her personality, a growing up. I put her into the same suspended animation I had used with others, delved into her mind with my omnipotence and straightened out the quirks there, brought her swiftly to her full human potential.

I woke her.

And I sorrowed.

Her full human potential was not enough.

She was strikingly beautiful, filled with a sensuality that made my loins stir, that would make any man sit up and take full notice of her. She was the essence of femininity, full-breasted, round-hipped, and long-legged, with honey hair and wide eyes, full lips and quick pink tongue. But she was no more than that to me. Even a beautiful woman who outshines all other females is of no interest if her mind seems as sawdust and her words strike you as the rambling proclamations of an idiot.

And so she seemed to me: an idiot, a thing, a moving construct of flesh. But not a woman I loved.

"What's the matter?" she asked.

"Nothing," I said. It pained me even to be forced to speak. Couldn't she understand me, without verbalizations? Couldn't she eke out even a hint of my thoughts without my having to spell them out for her in clean, crisp words and phrases?

"Something is," she said.

"Nothing."

"You're so distant. I can't tell if you're really there or not."

Oh, God, oh, God, I moaned to myself. But there was no use in that. It didn't help to pray to myself.

"It's as if," she said, "it's not you inside there. Maybe Child has taken over. Maybe just a little part of him has."

"No," I said.

"But if Child had taken you over, he would make you say that to satisfy me, wouldn't he?"

I said nothing.

"So maybe that's it."

"No."

I was very weary, very old.

"Something, anyway," she said.

"Yes. Something."

"I haven't asked you how you got here? How did you shake the cops?" She was smiling through all of this, though her face belied her true feelings beyond those brightly flashing teeth.

I did not answer her. I merely looked at her with a deep and melancholy sense of loss. And with a fear of the future that was to be mine from this day forth.

I saw, now, why God had eventually lost all touch with reality, had stepped across the thin red line into utter madness. He had begun as a super-intelligent creature able to set the precarious movements of the universe in perfect harmony, able to structure the balance of all creation. But as time had passed, He grew introverted because of His lack of company. There was no one worthy of Him, equal to Him, and He had stagnated with this lack of personal conflict and motivations.

The same would happen to me in time. It might require millennia, but it would happen all the same. Some day, I would whirl across the universe from one dark point to the other, insane, and babbling, my manipulatory mechanisms unable to harness the great psychic energy inside of me.

"I think I'm afraid of you," she said.

"I'm afraid of me too," I said.

"What's happened?" she asked.

But there was no sense telling her. There was no way to convey the absolute emptiness of the eternity that stretched before me. I had wanted a woman all my life, wanted to be loved and to return that affection tenfold. And now that I had finally shaken off all the false notions which had kept me from having a love—the false notions had come true and I was right back where I had started from.

And there seemed no hope at all. It seemed I had lost her.

V

But I had not lost her.

Even as I resigned myself to the future that all gods must face, I realized how the problem could be resolved. I had not been thinking with the omniscience of a god, and now that I suddenly began to apply myself as fully as I could, an answer loomed immediately in sight. I should have realized that to God there are no insoluble problems.

Why, then, had the previous God gone mad? Why hadn't He done what I was about to do to solve His loneliness? I thought I knew the answer to that one. He had not considered this utter loneliness to be a debit; perhaps He had not realized, as His existence had grown more petty and introverted, that what He needed was someone with whom to converse, exchange viewpoints and outlooks and mental visions. And by the time He had understood, it was too late: He was crazy.

What I had in mind was singularly simple. I took her by the shoulders and drew her next to me, reached into her mind with all the force of my esp.

She tried to fight.

It was no good.

I held her, and I funneled into her half the booming godly energy which I had contained, until the two of us were gods, each one half a god compared to the one deity before.

Her mind burst with psychedelic visions.

I fought down the rejection her own personality threw up, and helped her integrate the white power of godhood into her own being. We stood there for a very long while, locked physically and mentally as the changes came to her as they had come to me.

And we parted.

She took my hand, tenderly.

We did not speak.

There was no need for speech.

Together, we left that room and that building and went forth to take command of the world. The altar candles would be lighted, the prayers of the multitudes begun, and the sacrificial lambs led to the butchering block.

We passed many years on a perfect earth, racing from it to the corners of the universe. We saw all the places that had existed in the shattered mirror of God's mental analogue that time so long ago when I had confronted Him inside Child's mutant husk.

There were worlds where trees grew ugly sores and bled on the ground.

There were worlds where the sky shattered around us, was resurrected a hundred times every hour.

We saw walking plants that had built civilization within the darkness of an alien jungle.

We saw stones that spoke and stars that felt real pain.

For ten thousand years, we roamed the corners of existence, learning what sort of kingdom we had inherited.

And one day, Melinda said, "I'm bored. I've seen it all."

"I agree," I agreed.

"Let's revive religion," she said. "Let's at least let the people know we exist. We can come to them in burning bushes and in talking doves, and at least that will be amusing."

"Sounds fine," I said.

And though we had ended the rivalries of religions, we went down to the earth and revived them. We brought forth temples and synagogues, churches and altars, and garish robes and bejeweled priests. We created hierarchies of worthless prelates, and we spoke our words to the masses through the mouths of men of less value than most other men.

And for a time, that was fine, rather like camp culture. But soon the novelty of it wore off—like camp culture too.

"I'm bored," she said.

"Me too."

"But what is left?" she asked.

"We could stir things up a bit," I said.

"Stir things?"

"A war or two. Some killings. We could take sides. You could command the Southern Hemisphere, and I the North. And the winner—yes, I've got it! The winner will be permitted to expend enough energy to create a new race of beings on some far-flung world!"

"Marvelous!" she said, clasping her perfect hands across the full, rounded breasts I had come to know so well.

We had long ago learned that the energy required to create a race of beings or to form a new planet was too much of a drain on us. We required five centuries of recuperation from such a task, and recuperation meant boredom—which we could not afford.

It was a grand prize, then.

And the wars began. They still rage, for she is a formidable opponent, though I do believe I will eventually whip her Hemisphere with a contingent of laser-weaponed soldiers I have been concealing in a state of suspended animation beneath the North Pole. They are members of the Canadian army, well-trained and deadly. She does not know of them.

We have a fine time.

We play our games, battling for the grand prize, both of us already imagining what interesting and grotesque race we could create if permitted the use of the power.

We have a fine time.

On earth, men die, thrown at each other by our machinations. Some fleeting moments, when I am waiting for her to make her move, I consider my origins: made of men. I consider my life and Harry Kelly and Morsfagen and the lot of them. And then I consider what I am doing, and the old darkness in my soul returns. But not for long, of course. I am no fool. Morsfagen is dead. The society we knew has fallen to newer ones. Harry is long ago gone. I barely remember what he looked like. So we play our games and forget our doubts. Gods can have no doubts, as I said once before.

We play our games.

We have a fine time.

And now

DONALD A. WOLLHEIM

presents

The 1972 Annual World's Best SF

The continuation of the leading series of annual best of the world selections is now brought you by DAW BOOKS, and features the outstanding science fiction stories and novelettes from America, England, and the rest of the world.

Among the authors are:

> LARRY NIVEN
> ARTHUR C. CLARKE
> POUL ANDERSON
> THEODORE STURGEON
> HARLAN ELLISON
> STEPHEN TALL
> CHRISTOPHER PRIEST
> and many others.

The best sf buy of the year!

(#UQ1005—95¢)

Order by mail through the New American Library, Inc., the sales representatives of DAW BOOKS. Utilize coupon on ad pages for your convenience.

Do not miss any of the great science fiction from this exciting new paperback publisher!

- ☐ **TACTICS OF MISTAKE** by Gordon R. Dickson. An interstellar chess game played with living men and planets is the foundation of Dickson's Dorsai cosmos.
  (#UQ1009—95¢)

- ☐ **AT THE SEVENTH LEVEL** by Suzette Haden Elgin. Sexual chauvinism was the basis for that world's social structure—until the galaxy itself complained.
  (#UQ1010—95¢)

- ☐ **THE DAY BEFORE TOMORROW** by Gerard Klein. To dominate the future—change the past! A prize novel by the Ray Bradbury of France. (#UQ1011—95¢)

- ☐ **A DARKNESS IN MY SOUL** by Dean R. Koontz. The gene-tamperers produced two supermen—one a defiant mentalist, the other a defiant . . . god?
  (#UQ1012—95¢)

Four new SF books each month by the best of the SF authors. Ask your favorite local paperback book shop or newsdealer for DAW BOOKS.

DAW BOOKS are represented by the publishers of Signet and Mentor Books, THE NEW AMERICAN LIBRARY, INC.

THE NEW AMERICAN LIBRARY, INC.
P.O. Box 999, Bergenfield, New Jersey 07621

Please send me the DAW BOOKS I have checked above. I am enclosing $_____ (check or money order—no currency or C.O.D.'s). Please include the list price plus 15¢ a copy to cover mailing costs.

Name_____

Address_____

City_____ State_____ Zip_____

Please allow about 3 weeks for delivery

Do not miss any of the great science fiction from this exciting new paperback publisher!

☐ **THE 1972 ANNUAL WORLD'S BEST SF Edited by Donald A. Wollheim,** and presenting the finest science fiction stories of the year in one great anthology; including Clarke, Sturgeon, Niven, Anderson, etc.
(#UQ1005—95¢)

☐ **THE DAY STAR by Mark S. Geston.** In the sunset of humanity, they set out to reconstruct the glories of Earth's finest hour. (#UQ1006—95¢)

☐ **TO CHALLENGE CHAOS by Brian M. Stableford.** Last trip out to the only planet that spanned the two universes and two opposing laws of physics.
(#UQ1007—95¢)

☐ **THE MINDBLOCKED MAN by Jeff Sutton.** Manhunt in the 22nd Century—with a Solar Empire at stake.
(#UQ1008—95¢)

Four new SF books each month by the best of the SF authors. Ask your favorite local paperback book shop or newsdealer for DAW BOOKS.

DAW BOOKS are represented by the publishers of Signet and Mentor Books, THE NEW AMERICAN LIBRARY, INC.

THE NEW AMERICAN LIBRARY, INC.
P.O. Box 999, Bergenfield, New Jersey 07621

Please send me the DAW BOOKS I have checked above. I am enclosing $_____(check or money order—no currency or C.O.D.'s). Please include the list price plus 15¢ a copy to cover mailing costs.

Name_____

Address_____

City_____State_____Zip_____
Please allow about 3 weeks for delivery

Do not miss any of the great science fiction from this exciting new paperback publisher!

- [ ] **SPELL OF THE WITCH WORLD** by Andre Norton. The long-awaited new extra-galactic adventure by America's fastest selling SF author. (#UQ1001—95¢)

- [ ] **THE MIND BEHIND THE EYE** by Joseph Green. A giant's body is directed by an Earthly genius on an interstellar espionage mission. "A tour de force of the imagination"—Times (#UQ1002—95¢)

- [ ] **THE PROBABILITY MAN** by Brian N. Ball. The man of a thousand life-roles goes to unravel the secrets of a planet older than our universe. (#UQ1003—95¢)

- [ ] **THE BOOK OF VAN VOGT** by A. E. van Vogt. A brand new collection of original and never-before anthologized novelettes and tales by this leading SF writer.
  (#UQ1004—95¢)

Four new SF books each month by the best of the SF authors. Ask your favorite local paperback book shop or newsdealer for DAW BOOKS.

DAW BOOKS are represented by the publishers of Signet and Mentor Books, THE NEW AMERICAN LIBRARY, INC.

THE NEW AMERICAN LIBRARY, INC.
P.O. Box 999, Bergenfield, New Jersey 07621

Please send me the DAW BOOKS I have checked above. I am enclosing $_____ (check or money order—no currency or C.O.D.'s). Please include the list price plus 15¢ a copy to cover mailing costs.

Name_____

Address_____

City_____ State_____ Zip_____

Please allow about 3 weeks for delivery